THE GIRL WHO BECAME

A BEATLE

THE GIRL WHO BECAME
A BEATLE

GREG TAYLOR

FEIWEL AND FRIENDS
NEW YORK

A FEIWEL AND FRIENDS BOOK
An Imprint of Macmillan

Distributed in Canada by H.B. Fenn and Company Ltd.
Printed in January 2011 in the United States of America by R. R.
Donnelley & Sons Company, Harrisonburg, Virginia.
For information, address
Feiwel and Friends, 175 Fifth Avenue, New York, N.Y. 10010.

Library of Congress Cataloging-in-Publication Data

Taylor, Greg,
The girl who became a Beatle / Greg Taylor. — 1st ed.
p. cm.
Summary: Regina Bloomsbury, a sixteen-year-old,
Beatles-obsessed rocker, takes a trip to an alternate reality
where the Beatles never existed and her band, the Caverns,
are the rock-and-roll superstars.
ISBN: 978-0-312-65259-3 (hardcover) —
ISBN: 978-0-312-60683-1 (pbk.)
[1. Space and time—Fiction. 2. Fame—Fiction. 3. Rock
music—Fiction. 4. Beatles—Fiction. 5. Conduct of life—
Fiction.] I. Title.
PZ7.T21345Gi 2011
[Fic]—dc22
2010041450

Book design by Liz Herzog

Feiwel and Friends logo designed by Filomena Tuosto

First Edition: 2011

10 9 8 7 6 5 4 3 2 1

www.feiwelandfriends.com

BEATLES, THE, British musical ensemble whose innovations brought unprecedented sophistication to rock music, and who symbolized the personal and political rebellion and search for identity of many adolescents and young adults of the 1960s. Formed in 1960 and dissolved in 1970, the group consisted of four Liverpool-born musicians: George Harrison (1943–2001); John Winston Lennon (1940–80); (James) Paul McCartney (1942–); and, after 1962, Ringo Starr (1940–), whose real name is Richard Starkey and who replaced Peter Best, an original member of the group. From the simple, fresh style of early songs such as "I Want to Hold Your Hand" (1962), the Beatles progressed to innovative, experimental works such as the album *Sgt. Pepper's Lonely Hearts Club Band* (1967), admired for its dramatic unity, haunting harmony and lyrics, asymmetrical musical phrases and rhythms, and integrated use of electronic music techniques and Indian sitar sound. *See also* ROCK MUSIC.

—FUNK & WAGNALLS NEW ENCYCLOPEDIA,
Volume 3

OK, enough of the encyclopedia description of the Beatles.
My description?

BEATLES, THE, *Only one of the coolest, best, and most fun bands to ever hit the planet!*

Good. Now we can move on. . . .

PROLOGUE
An invitation

OK, I know you probably won't believe what you're about to read, but I swear it happened. It really did. The question is . . . how? *How* did it happen?

I've thought a lot about that question. There was of course the tossed-off wish I made after a particularly bad day. But this is the conclusion I've come to, as far as the *how* and *why* and *whatever* of all of this. Trying to explain anything truly magical is impossible. Best leave it a mystery.

So, if you're a rational kind of person who has a problem with fractured modern-day fairy tales, off-kilter faraway lands (in this case, Los Angeles), and wishes coming true (although not quite in the way you wished for), you probably shouldn't read any further. But if you're willing to suspend logic and believe, by all means . . . welcome aboard.

I'll admit that I'm writing this for myself as much as anyone. I'm afraid if I don't put down the entire story, very soon, I'll wake up some morning and all memory of my adventures will have vanished overnight. It'll be like it just never happened. And I can't allow that. One thing I'm very sure of here: I need to remember this journey. Too much important stuff went on to just let it disappear.

So let's get things started, shall we?

Once upon a time, not so very long ago, in a place called Twin Oaks in the northeastern United States . . .

PART ONE

Twin Oaks

1

A lot of winter days in Twin Oaks are like some of the black-and-white movies I've seen. Dreary, colorless, a total drag. (*A Hard Day's Night* does not fall into this category, of course.)

The morning of the day that I made my wish . . . was not like that. As my eyes fluttered open, I could tell it was going to be bright and sunny. Unfortunately, that did nothing to soothe my anxious state.

My uptightness was not unusual. Most mornings I wake up with the same feeling in my gut. Kind of queasy. Like I'm not on solid ground. Like something is unresolved in my life.

So what was it that morning? Did I neglect to study for a test? Was someone mad at me at school for some reason? When I stumbled into the bathroom, I got to the bottom of this mystery.

There it was, staring back at me from the mirror. No, not my *face*. Well, come to think of it, that's a good place to start. I'm not all that confident about how I look. But I don't want to get into that right now.

So no, actually, it was the words on the mirror that cracked this little puzzle for me. Sometimes I write reminders on the mirror in lipstick. And what was there this morning was this:

BE FIRM. DO NOT TAKE NO FOR AN ANSWER.

Explanation . . .

I play guitar and sing lead vocals for a band called the Caverns. We're a pop band, I'm proud to say. Mostly retro. Sixties British Invasion covers (more than a few Beatles songs, of course), a smattering of tunes from some of the smarter, newer pop groups, and—to keep things interesting—a few originals thrown in here and there. (None of mine, however. I'm kind of shy about playing my own stuff for people.)

I formed the Caverns during the summer. So far, we've only played a handful of gigs. A couple of times at the local coffee shop, a Battle of the Bands at our high school. A street fair near my house. So, we're kind of a new band, which makes me a bit uptight sometimes about the whole enterprise. It's like when you've just started dating someone and you're not sure where things are headed.

Anyway, back to that message on the mirror. As it turns out, my anxiety about the band was justified. Julian, our lead guitarist, had told me just the previous day that the Circuit Club—a hugely popular band at my school and one that has played a lot more gigs than the Caverns—was interested in Danny, our drummer, and Lorna, our bass player. As if that wasn't bad enough, it seemed that D and L were seriously thinking of accepting the evil band's offer!

So *that's* what my mirror-mirror-on-the-wall lipstick

message was all about. "Be firm. Do not take no for an answer" referred to my begging Mrs. Densby, head of the Entertainment Committee at T.J. High, to let the Caverns play at the Back to School dance, which would be happening right after Christmas break. I figured if I could get the gig—which would not only be the biggest one we'd played so far, but would actually pay us something—it might prevent my fidgety bandmates from bolting for Circuit Club. One gig, that is what I was desperate for. Then I'd take it from there.

"Regina! Breakfast!"

That's my dad. The human clock. He yells those same two words at exactly 6:30 a.m. every school day. I kid you not. Another annoying thing about him is that he's a morning person. Which is something I'm certainly not.

Unfortunately, I can't avoid Dad in the a.m. He teaches music at my school. So not only do I have to listen to him chatter away as we eat breakfast (he insists we eat together every morning) but on the way to school, too.

I have to admit, Dad and I have a complicated relationship. Mom left us years ago. As a result, Dad is . . . overly protective, I guess you could say. I'm sixteen years old and trying to spread my wings a bit, right? Not untypical. Meanwhile, Dad is doing his best to keep them clipped. Also not untypical. The point is, our diametrically opposed viewpoints on this particular issue leads to more than a little tension between us.

Don't get me wrong. I love Mister B, as the students call him. For one thing, Dad's the reason I'm such a Beatles nerd. He gave me *Meet the Beatles!* (on vinyl) for my twelfth birthday, and I've been hooked on them ever since. So I owe him. But *still*, a girl needs her space. Especially in the morning. But my space, as usual, was about to be invaded.

"What's the cryptic lipstick message all about, kiddo?" Dad looked at me over the glasses he needs to read the morning paper.

"Nothing," I replied, instantly defensive.

"Anything I can help you with?"

"No."

Dad got that wary look in his eyes. I had been shutting him out more and more lately.

"Look, Dad, sometimes a girl needs to figure things out on her own. OK?" Dad looked concerned. But he gave me a reluctant nod.

He was uncharacteristically quiet on the way to school. Which was fine with me. It gave me time to figure out what I was going to say to Mrs. Densby. I didn't want to improvise this very important conversation. It had to be totally worked out.

So work it out I did as Dad drove silently through the peaceful, eternally slumbering suburban streets of Twin Oaks. By the time I entered the teeming halls of Thomas Jefferson High, I had my pitch memorized. That made me feel a little better, but there was still one very important thing I had to do before talking to Mrs. Densby.

Avoid my bandmates. That way they couldn't even broach the subject of breaking up the Caverns. Ducking Danny and Lorna wouldn't be difficult. They're a grade below me, so I didn't have any classes with them. But Julian was a different matter. We have the same math class and share the same homeroom. Most days, that's good. Because, well, I guess it's time to tell you about Julian and me.

I'm in love with him. He's not in love with me.

Sorry. I know that's so . . . typical. Unrequited love and all. At least I'm pretty sure it's unrequited. Julian and I really get along, is the thing. We have a similar sense of humor. Kind of *off*, if you know what I mean. We like the same kinds of songs, of course. We sometimes finish each other's sentences. I like it when that happens because that tells me we're totally on the same wavelength.

All that said, what Julian and I have between us feels like a friends kind of vibe. So I've always been afraid to let Julian know how I really feel about him, because that might spoil what we already have.

Now you know one of the main reasons why I was so intent on preventing the Caverns from breaking up. I'm not sure if Julian and I would even see each other very much anymore. It could be the only reason we were friends was because we were in a band together. Take away the band . . . there goes Julian. And any chance for me to ever get up the nerve to tell him how I really feel about him.

Speaking of the boy, here he was. As soon as I entered my homeroom and sat down at my desk, he was standing right next to me.

"We gotta talk, Gina." Julian wore his hair in a classic Beatles cut and dressed '60s-style. Which made him all that more irresistible to me.

"I wouldn't get too close, Julian. I'm . . . getting sick."

"You're the worst liar in the world. All I have to do is look in your eyes."

I didn't want to look in his. He has really terrific blue-green eyes. Soulful eyes. You could get lost in those eyes. As for mine,

I put sunglasses on. (I always have a pair on hand, even in winter, just in case I want to look mysterious. Or *inscrutable*, I believe is the word.)

"I have to study," I said.

"It's the last day before Christmas break. What do you have to study for?"

"SATs," I lied. Well, I was taking them sometime early in the New Year, but with my current crisis, I didn't really care about them.

"Danny and Lorna want to meet during lunch," Julian said.

"I can't. I have to—"

"If they're gonna quit, it's better to know sooner than later, don't you think?"

I didn't want to answer that question. So I didn't.

"C'mon, Gina, it's not the end of the world. There are plenty of musicians out there. You can put a new band together."

My heart sank. Because Julian had said "you," not "we."

"You sound like it's a done deal," I said. I wasn't looking at him when I said it. Julian slowly removed my sunglasses. I glanced sideways at him. He looked kind of sad. Which told me he knew it was a done deal. "I gotta get back to . . . this," I said lamely. And quickly put my sunglasses back on. Because I didn't want Julian to see me cry.

Can you believe it? Tears first thing in the a.m. I couldn't help it, however. The Caverns really did mean that much to me. Julian, Lorna, and Danny were my tribe, after all. The band was my identity. In the bizarre, surreal world called high school, the Caverns was my lifeline to sanity.

So that was one reason I started to lose it in homeroom class the morning of the day that I made my wish. The other reason was . . . I didn't think I was that great of a musician. Or singer. Or songwriter. And I figured that's why Danny and Lorna and Julian really wanted to break up the band. I wasn't good enough. Plain and simple.

Maybe everyone at my age has these kind of doubts. For those of you who don't, let me tell you, they can paralyze you. Just stop you in your tracks. Give you panic attacks.

My way of dealing with them was to keep moving. Like a shark. Keep practicing. Keep writing songs (even though nobody ever heard them). Keep trying to get gigs. That helped keep my insecurities at bay. But sometimes they took over.

This was one of those times. Julian, bless him, knew not to push it. He gave me a pat on the arm and said, "We'll talk later." I couldn't get any words out because of the lump in my throat. So I just nodded.

That's how my day started. And it would only get worse from there.

2

"Hi, Mrs. Densby."

I had managed to pull myself together and plaster a fake can-do smile across my face before approaching Mrs. Densby at the front of the auditorium. She had study hall second period, so I figured that was the best time to talk to her about the dance. The smile was meant to cover up the fact that my heart was beating like a hummingbird's.

"Hello, Regina. What can I do for you?"

"You can let the Caverns play at the Back to School dance."

Hmmm. That wasn't what I'd rehearsed, what I'd memorized on the way to school. I was going to break the ice with some small talk. Compliment her on her strange-looking outfit (she always wore weird ensembles that screamed, "Color-coordinated!"). But before I could stop myself, I had eliminated the preliminaries and cut right to the heart of the matter. It seemed to catch Mrs. Densby off guard. She took a moment to consider the question.

"Well, you see, I can't do that, Regina. DJ Jimmy already has the job."

DJs! Besides Circuit Club, the bane of my existence. What

was so special about DJs? Why did everyone want them instead of real, live music these days? At the school dances. At the pool parties in the summer. At the frat parties over at the college. Those were all places my dad had played with the Lost Souls, his high school band.

That was back in the day, that's for sure. The Golden Era, the Shangri-La, the Camelot for garage bands. I feel like I was born thirty years too late. Because today the DJs ruled. And they were strangling the Caverns. Taking all the gigs away from us.

"DJ Jimmy always gets the gigs," I said. "The ones he doesn't play, Circuit Club does. Why not do something different for a change?" I was aware that my voice went up a notch as I talked. Not a good sign. Another pitch and I'd be whining.

"Tell you what I'll do," Mrs. Densby said. "I'll put that suggestion before the committee."

"But that means the next dance. And that's not until next spring!" There it was. I had crossed the border into Whiny Burg with those last two words. I have terrible self-control.

"You kids are always in a hurry, aren't you?" Mrs. Densby leaned casually back in her chair. The look on her face seemed to say, *Wait until you get to my age. You'll learn to take life nice and easy.*

It was all I could do not to grab her by her purple lapels, shake her, and scream, *Yes! You betcha I'm in a hurry! My life depends on this!*

But I didn't. I took a deep breath, then, as calmly as possible, said, "I really wish you would reconsider about the upcoming Back to School dance, Mrs. Densby."

Mrs. Densby took off her glasses, which made my heart sink. 'Cause that's what my dad always did when we were about to have a heart-to-heart.

"Regina, I think it's wonderful that you are so devoted to your band." See, I knew it. "And you mustn't give up. I heard you play at that Battle of the Bands at the beginning of the school year." (The one we lost to Circuit Club.) "And I have to say, I thought you were really good. Especially those Beatles songs."

I gritted my teeth and said, "Thank you."

"Anything else, Regina?"

She'd already dismissed me. I could tell. Her mind was somewhere else. Where, I didn't want to know.

"No, that's it," I said meekly. (As my inner voice screamed, *"Hey, what happened to 'Be firm. Do not take no for an answer?' Huh? What happened?!!!"*)

Just then a paper airplane sailed over our heads and landed on the stage behind Mrs. Densby's desk. Giggles erupted behind me.

"Enough of that! This is *study hall!*" It was not a pretty sight to see Mrs. Densby morph from the Understanding Teacher into the Purple General. So I got out of there, fast. Besides, the bell was ringing, which meant I was going to be late for math class.

But really, at that point I didn't care. My one shot at keeping the band alive had been delivered a fatal blow. My Save the Band campaign was over.

Fortunately, as I dragged my carcass around a corner in the hallway, a ray of light streaming through a high window blasted me flush in the face. It was like being hit with divine inspiration.

I stopped suddenly and smiled up at the glorious light. *What on earth is wrong with you?* I scolded myself. This wasn't the only gig in town. Close to it, but not the *only* one.

There was the VFW, for instance, which sometimes hosted theme dances. True, no one my age would be caught dead in the place, but so what? I would go there right after school and tell them that what they absolutely *had to have* for the holidays was a Back to the '60s dance.

If that didn't work, I'd ask Dad to throw a Christmas party for all of his friends (I think he had some). The Caverns could entertain the guests, of course.

Then there was . . . well, I wasn't sure what else there was, but I'd think of something.

It ain't over till it's over, I thought. Then I practically skipped down the hall with renewed hope and energy.

(Are all teenagers like this? Ricocheting from despair to euphoria within one turn of the minute hand? If so, no wonder we're always so exhausted!)

Math, the class I was late for, was the one I had with Julian. I was bursting to tell him about all of my gig ideas but figured it might be best to just surprise him. Besides, when we made eye contact a couple of times, I got the impression he didn't really want to talk to me. Maybe because of my emo display in the morning. That kind of thing can make a guy uncomfortable. So we sidestepped each other after class, and I managed to avoid a confrontation with Lorna and Danny by not going to lunch.

As I stood at my locker at the end of the school day—with all the crazy energy swirling around me, that special energy that can only come from a rambunctious group of schoolkids just before a long vacation—I had convinced myself the Caverns (and hence, Julian and me) still had a chance. And I couldn't wait to get to the VFW and *make magic happen*!

"Regina?"

I froze. That unmistakable voice could come from only one person.

Lorna.

I pretended not to hear her. That way, maybe she'd just go away. Eventually. But she wasn't going away. I knew that. I just didn't want to believe it.

Lorna leaned against the locker next to mine. She's a cool-looking girl and a classic cynic. We hadn't known each other all that well before she tried out for the band. Still, like most kids in my school, I had certainly known *of* Lorna. That's because she'd always had a pretty wild rep. The whole punk, dressed-in-black thing? Lorna had blasted through that before she'd even hit her teenage years. Even though that wasn't her deal anymore, she still had a prickly personality and looked at the world through black-tinted glasses to a certain extent. She looked at me now, poker-faced.

"You've been a tough girl to find," she said.

"I've been busy."

"You've been avoiding me."

"And me," Danny piped in from behind.

I turned to face Danny. Normally, he's all smiles and high fives. He's like a human pinball. Talks a mile a minute and plays the drums like a madman. Think ADD ten-year-old in a fifteen-year-old body, and you've got the idea. Underneath all that hyper-energy, though, Danny's a really sweet guy and Lorna's opposite, personality-wise.

"Listen, guys, I've got some great ideas for gigs. I just need a little time. . . ."

"That's what you said last month," Lorna said. "*Two* months ago, you said that."

"All we ever do is practice," Danny added. It sounded rehearsed, what they were saying. And it really bugged me that Lorna was obviously the one who had been in charge of the rehearsal. Danny seemed like her puppet or something. Still, I had to be nice to Lorna. I needed her in the band. If she went, I had no doubt Danny would follow right behind her.

"Speaking of practicing, you guys are coming over tonight, right? It'll be fun. We'll kick off the holiday with some new tunes, and . . ."

"We're not coming over, Regina." Lorna didn't have a problem getting right to it. Danny looked at the linoleum floor. He wasn't big on confrontation.

"Why not?" I asked, as innocently as I could.

"C'mon, Regina. Julian must have told you."

"He said you might be joining Circuit Club. *Might* being the operative word here. I thought that meant I had a little time to get some gigs and—"

Interrupting my plea for patience, Lorna said in a bored, monotone voice, "You know what? I'm getting tired of the whole sixties thing, anyway."

Tired of '60s music! That was blasphemous, of course.

But I checked my anger and tried to channel it. "So you'd rather play with some techno . . . rap . . . heavy-metal band? Is that it?"

"At least they play for people once in a while. And get paid for it."

I was aware that a small group had gathered across the hallway and were staring at us. Someone whispered, "Catfight!"

"We'll talk about this tonight," I said in desperation.

"Didn't you hear anything we said?"

"I did, but I suggest you think it over a bit."

"We've been thinking about this for months. We're tired of thinking about it. We're tired of practicing all the time and never playing for anyone. It's a drag." Lorna looked at Danny for some backup. Danny glanced at me, helplessly, then went back to studying the pattern on the floor.

Before I knew what I was doing, I slammed my locker and walked off down the hallway.

"You can't just walk away like this, Regina," Lorna said in an angry, louder voice, drawing even more attention from the crowd.

I didn't respond. Tears were suddenly blinding my vision. The exit doors swam in a blur at the far end of the hall. If I could just get through those doors, I'd be OK. That's what I convinced myself.

"OK, we quit," Lorna yelled. "Is that what you needed to hear to make it official?"

It was. That single word was like a knife in my heart.

That's when I tripped. Maybe it was the fatal word, *quit*.

Maybe it was the blinding tears. Maybe both. But the rubber toe of my sneaker caught on the hallway floor at that precise moment, and I tumbled forward and hit the deck.

Picture that. With everyone watching . . . *splat!* Right on my face. Totally humiliated, I leaped to my feet and ran off down the hallway. I could hear some people laugh as I pushed through the doors and escaped outside.

I found a private spot on the other side of the football field before I gave in to a total breakdown. For the second time in the course of that misbegotten day, I lost it. But this one was a gusher compared to the one in homeroom.

I know what you're thinking. What a nutty gal. Or a case of overreacting hormones, at the very least. But the pain I felt was real, believe me. It was like I'd been hit in the gut and all the air had escaped from inside me. And as I sat behind the football field on the wet grass, I knew it was time to accept the inevitable.

The band was over. It really was. Just like that, my tribe had been reduced to a grand total of . . .

One.

3

I didn't take the bus home or hitch a ride with Dad. What was the hurry? The band wasn't practicing later like we'd planned. I didn't need to rush off to the VFW to try to get a holiday gig. So I walked home.

It's a long walk, along a two laner that goes past a few farms and some new 'burban sprawls. That was good, because it gave me plenty of time to consider where I was going to run away to.

I had considered . . .

(A) New York (great for disappearing into a crowd)

(B) Peru (I had seen this intense film about these two guys who almost died trying to *get down* from a mountain. Right now, that sounded incredibly romantic to me for some reason.)

(C) California (That's where my mom lived.)

(D) England (Of course! Why didn't I think of that first?)

. . . by the time I turned onto my street.

The final half block to 489 Lynn Drive was the hardest

part of my trek home. My legs suddenly felt like they had fifty-pound weights on them. It was all I could do to put one foot in front of the other. It wasn't because I was tired.

I just . . .
(three houses away)
. . . didn't . . .
(two houses away)
. . . want . . .
(one house away)
. . . to see . . .
(going up the steps to the front door)
. . . or talk . . .
(opening the front door)
. . . to *anyone*.

My dad especially. I knew he'd zone in on how bad I was feeling. He had an uncanny ability to do that. And I didn't want to have one of those heart-to-hearts I mentioned, because they were always awkward.

That's because that was Mom's domain. Before she left. Not that she was all that good at it. But it did fall into her territory. And whenever Dad tried to tread on what used to be Mom Territory, I know it made him think of her, which made him feel bad. And it made me think of her, too, which made *me* feel bad.

So the very purpose of the heart-to-heart—which was to make me feel better—was always negated by the bad feelings that were conjured up by remembering those days. When Mom still lived with us. And cared about us.

It sounds complicated, I know. That's because it is. Which is why I figured I'd duck right past Dad and head to my bedroom. Where I'd pack for my trip to England.

But when I came into the house and headed quickly for the stairs, "Let It Be" was playing on the stereo. Looking back on it, it does seem kinda like fate that Dad was playing a Beatles song at that specific point in time. Paul's lyrics, those wonderful lyrics, stopped me right in my tracks. They seemed to wash over me, instantly soothing my hyperactive, anxious state. As though in a trance, I sat on the sofa, heavy winter jacket still on, the packed snow from the treads of my boots melting into the rug, and listened until I heard, *"There will be an answer, / Let it be."*

By then Dad had appeared and was standing by the Christmas tree, which we'd bought, set up, and decorated just a few days before. He had a loopy sort of smile on his face, the kind he always got when he'd just heard some really great music.

"One of the best songs ever, isn't it, kiddo?"

I didn't respond. That's because I wasn't in the living room anymore.

Explanation . . .

Dad often asks me, "Regina, where are you now?" That's when he catches me off in my own world. Daydreaming, some people would call it. Regina's World is what my dad calls it. A mysterious place, more often than not. A place with mental signposts on the perimeter that read RESTRICTED and NO ENTRY. A place where I spend maybe a little too much time, to be honest. And that freaked Dad out. 'Cause he thought that was my way of avoiding the real world.

Which maybe it was.

Anyway, that's where I was. In Regina's World. With the Beatles. And this is when I made my wish. That tossed-off wish I told you about.

"I wish I were as famous as the Beatles."

It's sad and kind of embarrassing to admit I said that. But it's also understandable why I uttered those fateful words. That kind of fame would take care of all my problems, right?

Boy problems: Check.

Self-confidence problems: Check.

Tribe-of-one problems: Check.

I hardly noticed it at the time, probably because I was so zoned out on how bad I was feeling, but a weird thing happened right after I made my wish. It felt like there was a little hiccup in time, is the best way I can put it. Like, if I was watching myself and Dad on a video playback, I'd see our image suddenly jump back a few seconds and play the same scene over again. A weird sensation, it was, but I shook it off and headed for the stairs.

"Where are you going, Regina?" Dad looked concerned. I couldn't blame him. The words he just heard me say clearly did not come from someone who was on top of the world.

"Where do you think, Dad? What's on the second floor besides your bedroom and the bathroom?" I knew that was nasty and sarcastic even as I said it. And I hated myself for it.

"What's wrong, honey?"

"Nothing."

"Does it have something to do with that message on the mirror this morning?"

"I don't want to talk about it."

"Sometimes it's good to talk. To get things out."

"Right, and then you'll tell me to just hang in there. Because wonderful is just around the corner. And then you'll say how awkward the teen years are. And how it takes time to become the person you're going to be. But I don't want to hear that. I want things to be wonderful right now, you know? Sometimes I get tired of waiting for wonderful!"

My room was almost dark when I came in and closed the door. It was only four o'clock, but the light outside was already beginning to fade. That's when I remembered. It was December 21. The shortest day of the year. Somehow that seemed perfect, considering everything that had happened today.

Without turning on any lights, I got into bed and curled myself up into a ball. I lay motionless under the covers, surrounded by the comforting cocoon of my room.

I have been an ardent collector of Beatles paraphernalia ever since Dad gave me the *Meet the Beatles!* album.

Posters. Dolls. Books. Lunch boxes. A nine-by-three-inch black-and-yellow ticket with the Fab Four's smiling faces on it that my dad got when he went to see *A Hard Day's Night* in 1965 at the Echo Drive-In.

And, of course, there was my original *Meet the Beatles!* album cover, framed and hanging over my bed, with John, Paul, George, and Ringo's eternally cool, unsmiling, half-in-shadow faces staring moodily at the camera.

Don't get me wrong. I listen to all kinds of music. But let's face it, the Beatles are special. They're in a class of their own.

So that's what surrounded me as I desperately sought the oblivion of sleep. Dozens of Beatles visages. They watched over me until I eventually nodded off. Without having any dinner. Without changing my clothes. Or brushing my teeth. Or doing any of the other things you would normally do on a typical winter evening in Twin Oaks. Because when you felt as miserable as I did, mundane things like eating didn't seem so important.

However, as I drifted off to the sound track of my stomach making all kinds of strange noises, little did I know that things were about to change for me, and fast. Yes, ladies and gents, it would be a completely different ball game when the sun came up in the morning, leaving the shortest day of the year in its wake.

Because, as it turned out, I wouldn't have to wait long, after all.

For wonderful, that is.

4

"C'mon, Regina. They're going to be here before you know it."

Dad stood next to my bed, shaking my shoulder. Being in a rather catatonic state, I stared blankly back at him. Let's face it, when you've slept for more than twelve hours, it's harder than usual to wake up. It's like there's an extra layer of *stuff* around your brain and you have to push through it to become a somewhat-functioning human being again.

"Who's gonna be here?" I mumbled.

"Very funny. This was your idea, remember?"

Dad opened the curtains. I think I screamed, it was so bright. I dove under the covers to shield myself from the glare.

"I'll be more than happy to tell them you're not feeling well. We can just play the concert and leave it at that."

What on earth was Dad talking about?

"Let me know what you want to do," he said as he walked out of the room.

I slowly inched up from under the covers, allowing my eyes to adjust to the light. I felt like I was being reborn or something. When I finally got out of bed, my eyes were still squinty.

All that light! So I went to the window and closed the curtains.

Better, I thought, then padded sleepily across the room. I made it to the hallway—on my way to the bathroom—before I stopped. Something had caught my eye on the shelf in my bedroom, but it had taken a few seconds to register.

I slowly retraced my steps back to the shelf. Yep, that's what I thought I had seen. But I still couldn't believe it. I blinked a few times, thinking that might make everything come into clearer focus.

It didn't. A mistake had not been made. I was still looking at what I thought I was looking at. OK, I won't keep you in suspense any longer. What I was looking at was . . .

A Regina Bloomsbury doll.

Ever see one of those Beatle dolls from the '60s? Four inches high. Made of rubber. Oversize heads. John, Paul, George, and Ringo, all wearing black Beatle suits. You can buy them on eBay. Well, the Regina doll looked just like those old Beatle dolls. Except that my rubber likeness wore a black turtleneck and black miniskirt, and the rubber guitar hanging around my neck read REGINA.

I stared dumbly at the Regina doll, still feeling kind of fuzzy in the head, and thought, *OK, this is strange.* Just as odd was the fact that my John, Paul, George, and Ringo Beatle dolls were not on the shelf where they had been the night before.

My eyes now wandered to the red plastic lunch box next to the Regina doll. The previous night, it had been a metal Beatles lunch box. Now it was . . .

A Caverns lunch box.

I looked closer. It was. It was a plastic Caverns lunch box.

That's when my heart started to do double time. Something was seriously wrong, I knew. I mean, here I was, staring at a picture of me, Julian, Lorna, and Danny on the side of that lunch box. We were all smiles and positioned just like the picture of the Beatles on that *Hard Day's Night* ticket I told you about.

Which was no longer hanging on my wall. In its place was a framed platinum record announcing—get this—that *Meet the Caverns!* had sold more than a million copies!

I literally staggered back a few steps when I saw that platinum album. The *Meet the Caverns!* cover looked exactly like the *Meet the Beatles!* album cover, except of course it was my face—along with Julian's, Lorna's, and Danny's—in half shadow instead of the Beatles'.

By this point I was light-headed. I really thought I would faint. I sat on the edge of my bed and stared around my room. *This is a joke*, I thought. *Dad took all my Beatles stuff and replaced it with the fake Caverns stuff.*

I rejected that idea as soon as I thought of it. Nobody could have pulled off a stunt like that overnight. Besides, why would anyone want to do such a thing?

No, the simple fact was that there was nothing Beatles-related left in my room. No Beatles posters or buttons or calendars or dolls or my set of miniature album covers— *Something New* and *Rubber Soul* and *Sgt. Pepper's* among them—with the bubble gum inside that looked like little, round pink albums. Everything that had been there the night before . . .

Gone.

In place of my beloved Beatles stuff was Caverns stuff. My entire room had been turned into a shrine to the supposedly multimillion-selling Caverns.

Suddenly, I laughed out loud. I did. How could I react any other way? What I was seeing was so absurd, how could I take it seriously?

A commotion outside interrupted my hilarity. It sounded like a lot of people. Strangely, some were yelling, "Regina!" I walked warily across the room and peeked through a corner windowpane.

Whoa! There were a lot of people out there. A crowd had gathered around a car and van parked by my front curb. Some of the people I recognized. Neighbors. But everyone else was a stranger. Some had cameras around their necks. Some held video cameras and microphones. There was an official-looking woman dressed in a long black overcoat and carrying a clipboard, who paced by the car talking on a cell phone.

The video-camera people, dressed in hip, colorful clothes, stood in front of the van. When they suddenly moved toward my house, I was able to see that *MTV* was printed on the door of the van.

That did it. This was no laughing matter anymore. Whatever strange magic was going on had already gone on long enough. So that's when I decided to freak out. I jumped back, pulled the curtain around me, and shouted, "DAD!" at the top of my lungs. Just like a frightened little girl, I needed my daddy.

5

It took Dad only a few seconds to respond to my cry for help. When he appeared at my door, I yelped, "What's going on here?"

Dad didn't answer. He looked too alarmed to respond to my question. For good reason, I suppose. I stood in the corner of my room with the curtain wrapped around me like a shroud. I must have looked like a total loon.

"Why does my room look like this?" I pleaded. "Why is MTV outside?"

Dad looked me up and down, then shook his head grimly. "I was afraid all of this would get to you, Regina. I told you to take it easier. Didn't I tell you that?"

"C'mon, Dad, stop goofin' around. I go to bed last night with all my Beatle stuff right where it should be. Then I wake up to . . . this?"

"Beatle stuff? What's that?"

The front doorbell rang. Dad and I stared at each other in uneasy silence. Finally, Dad said, "I'm going to tell them to just film the concert. None of this following you around all day. They can do that with the rest of the band."

Dad walked from the room. Then he ducked his head back in, just to be sure I hadn't collapsed or something. When he was satisfied I was sort of OK, he went off to deal with the MTV people. Which gave me a little time to try to sort all of this out.

My first thought was that I'd had some kind of weird break-down due to my band members' rejection the day before. Or I'd slipped into an alternate universe during the night while I was tossing and turning. Or, the easiest to comprehend, I was still tossing and turning and was actually dreaming all this.

Good. Done. That was the obvious explanation. I was simply dreaming. *Whew.* Explanation accepted.

Once I had convinced myself that the world around me was actually REM in the middle of the night, I calmed down a bit. But just a bit, to be honest. Because the world around me didn't really feel like dream. It felt real and sequential and in the moment. Not all jumbled and time-jumpy like dreams usually are. So I was still uneasy, but at least I was able to think in a somewhat-rational way.

First things first, I told myself. Which would be . . . what? *Well, unfurl yourself from this curtain.* Which I did. *Now what?* I wondered. As I looked around my room, the lack of anything Beatles-related was what intrigued me most. More so than even that *Meet the Caverns!* platinum album.

Beatles stuff? What's that?

That's what Dad had said when I mentioned the Beatles. It was like he'd never heard of them!

A thought impudently snapped its fingers inside my over-heated brain. *Good idea*, I congratulated myself. I went to my computer, logged on to the Net and Googled "The Beatles." I had used Google just a week or so before to find a Beatles-related Web site for song lyrics. At the time, there were over thirty million results from my Beatles Google. Now, the usually lightning-fast Google computers took a while to respond. Finally, a message came on the screen:

"There are no results related to this subject."

Incredible. Unbelievable. *Mind-boggling*. According to the World Wide Web—the ultimate authority—the Beatles simply did not exist in this new dreamworld of mine! I felt strangely calm about this revelation. Probably because I figured I would wake up at any moment and things would be back to normal.

Dad suddenly reappeared at my door. "They didn't like it, but they're leaving you alone until the concert."

"OK" is all I could think of to say.

"Seriously, Regina. How are you feeling?"

"Good. I mean, I had a bad dream. You know how I get those sometimes. Just freaked me out a bit."

"Maybe you should see a doctor."

"No, Dad. I'm fine." I smiled and did my best to imitate someone normal. Someone who wasn't groping her way through a dreamworld.

Dad looked like he wasn't buying it. But finally he said, "I'm making breakfast. Come on down when you're ready."

"I will." A final bit of scrutiny from Dad, then he turned and went downstairs. When I turned back to my computer, my mouth dropped when I saw what was on the screen.

"There are no results related to this subject" had been replaced with "This is not a dream. Your wish has been granted."

My wish? What wish? I thought.

Strange as it may seem, I hadn't connected all of this to the wish I had made the night before. Why would I? After all, it wasn't like I'd positioned a bunch of lit candles in a circle and made a formal request in the middle of them. (OK, I'll admit I'd done that before. But I was probably around six at the time.) My wish was just tossed off, like I said.

Now the words on the computer dissolved and were replaced with "Do you have any questions?"

I couldn't believe what I was seeing. I mean, who was this person on my computer?

That's a good question, I thought.

"Who are you?" I typed.

"Your Fairy Godmother" came the response.

My dream had obviously taken a very strange turn. I decided the best thing to do was continue the conversation. I typed, "How do I know you're not just part of my dream?"

"C'mon, Regina. Deep down you know you're not dreaming" was the reply from my faceless Fairy Godmother.

That hit me right in the gut. Because my so-called F.G. was right. I had tried to convince myself that my new world was a dream because it was the only rational explanation of what was going on. I mean, *wishes simply never came true!* None of mine had, anyway.

I quickly typed, "OK, let's say this isn't a dream. Let's pretend my wish has been granted. If so, there's been a big mistake. I wished to be as famous as the Beatles. Not make the Beatles disappear!"

"It's impossible to be as famous as the Beatles" came the

immediate response. "So I simply eliminated them and gave all their songs to you."

All their songs to me?

I stared at the computer in stunned silence. I hadn't thought about what was on *Meet the Caverns!* Things had been happening too fast for me to even get that far. I shoved away from the desk and caromed over to my CD cabinet on my rollable chair. When I found *Meet the Caverns!*, I extracted it from the cabinet and turned it over. This is what was on the back:

1. He Loves You

2. I Want to Hold Your Hand

3. Eight Days a Week

4. Please Please Me

5. All My Loving

6. Help!

7. We Can Work It Out

8. I Should Have Known Better

9. Yesterday

10. I'm a Loser

11. In My Life

12. Hello, Goodbye

Words and Music: Regina Bloomsbury

I stared for the longest time at the back of that CD. Part of me was psyched to see that every one of the songs was a personal favorite of mine. But there was another part of me that wondered . . . how did this person claiming to be my Fairy Godmother know what my favorite Beatles songs were?

I spun around in my chair and looked back at my computer. I had a lot of questions to ask this lady. But when I rolled back to my desk, I was stunned at what I saw on the screen:

"Gotta go. Much to do. Good luck."

WHAT!

I furiously typed, "Wait a second! I need to talk to you!"

No reply. I couldn't believe it. That was it? That was the end of our conversation?

What kind of Fairy Godmother is this? I thought as the words on the computer dissolved, leaving the screen blank. *Fairy Godmothers don't abandon their little princesses!*

I sat stock-still when I had that thought. I slowly looked around at all of the Caverns-related merchandise in my room. That's when it really hit me. Crystal clear. Right between the eyes.

This wasn't a dream after all. This was for real. My wish *had* been granted.

I had become a pop princess overnight.

6

"Have you packed for tomorrow?"

I was gobbling down my scrambled eggs when Dad asked me that question. I had wanted to crawl back into bed after my strange Fairy Godmother left me to deal with all this insanity by myself. But then I realized I was too famished to put off eating any longer. It had been almost twenty-four hours since I'd put anything in my stomach.

"Packing? Tomorrow?" I said absentmindedly.

"Slow down, Regina. You're going to get sick."

I polished off my eggs and grabbed another piece of toast. "Partly," I replied.

"Partly what?" Dad asked.

"Partly I'm done packing." I figured that was a safe reply to my dad's question.

Dad nodded, then stared out of the kitchen window. A cluster of young girls and a few paparazzi were gathered just on the other side of our property, waiting for me to make an appearance, the girls providing a constant refrain of "Regina!" A couple of the paparazzi started to edge closer to the house, I suppose to try to get a shot of me through the window or something.

Dad leaped to his feet, yanked open the kitchen door, and shouted, "Care to be arrested for trespassing on private property?"

The photographers immediately backed off, but not before snapping a couple of pictures of my dad. He slammed the door and returned to the table, muttering under his breath, his adjectives for the paparazzi obviously not meant to reach my innocent ears.

So, the paparazzi . . . Dad not a fan. I wasn't sure how I felt about them. Before my instant stardom, I'd seen them only on celebrity TV shows hounding movie and TV and music stars, and now here they were hounding me. Definitely weird, and kind of funny in a way. But they were more like background weirdness at that point in my rock 'n' roll journey. There was too much else to be concerned about.

"So . . . it's going to be an interesting week," Dad said, which took my mind off the waving hands and bobbing heads of my girl fans and the black-clad snappers out by the curb. Something was troubling Dad, I could tell, and I didn't think it was the paparazzi. But I didn't want to ask what it was. I needed more information first. About what was going on.

I mean, here this incredibly bizarre out-there *thing* had happened to me overnight. But from the looks of things, I was the only one who knew it had happened. Everyone else seemed to have been living for quite some time in this new pop diva world of mine . . . except me.

Confusing? You bet it was.

"I better go get ready for tomorrow," I said. Whatever tomorrow was. Before I left the kitchen, Dad asked, "You are coming back, aren't you?"

"Coming back? Here? To the kitchen?"

"You know what I'm talking about, Regina."

No, I didn't. *I didn't have the faintest clue what was going on!* Which was why I needed to get back to my room. Research. "We'll talk about this later, Dad." Again, a safe thing to say. At that point, I was just stalling for time. Until I had a clue.

Google led me to the Caverns' official Web site. A wealth of information greeted me. This is what I discovered:

Meet the Caverns! had already spawned three number-one hits. The next official single from the album was going to be "He Loves You."

The CD had sold over four million copies to date.

It had been nominated for a total of seven Grammy Awards, including Best Album, Best Song (for "Yesterday"), and Best Rock Album. Plus the band was up for Best New Artist.

We were close to completing our hotly awaited second album, which was going to be released in the spring.

To kick off Grammy week, the Caverns were playing a concert—which would be streamed on the MTV Web site to a worldwide audience—at our former high school, T.J. High in Twin Oaks, on February 9.

I looked at the Caverns calendar hanging on the wall by my desk. It was open to February. The first eight days of the month had been crossed off.

Interesting.

Apparently, I had traveled from December 21 to February 9 overnight. Which meant that the Grammys were in one week.

Aha!

That's what I was supposed to be packing for. A trip to L.A. to attend the Grammy Awards! But wait a second. It also meant that the Caverns concert at T.J. was . . .

Tonight!

My stomach jumped into hyperdrive when I was confronted with that info. I always get nervous when I perform. But nervous in a good way. This was nervous in a not-so-good way. I mean, I couldn't just stumble blindly through the day until concert time. That's what I felt like at that point.

Blind.

For one thing, what was with the announcement on our Web site that we were playing a concert at our *former* high school? Had we quit school?

I sighed in frustration. There was only so much I could learn from a Web site. Even an official one. I needed to discover what else was going on. Behind the scenes. I needed to fill in the details of my new life.

A confidant.

That's what I needed. Someone I could talk to. Someone I could trust. (Seeing as my lousy Fairy Godmother had abandoned me!) Someone I could maybe even tell the truth about what was really going on. Without them thinking I had bought a one-way ticket to Nutville. There was only one person I knew who fit that description.

Julian.

7

" 'Lo?" Julian answered his cell phone on the second ring.

"It's me, Regina."

"Gina. Heard you're not feeling well. What's wrong?"

I immediately tensed up when I heard Julian's voice. The vibe coming over the phone was weird. Off, in some way. But then I thought, *Probably just me. This is Julian, after all.*

"I'm just a little under the weather," I replied.

"You be OK for the concert?"

No, there it was again. A kind of flat, uninterested tone to Julian's voice. What was going on here?

"Yeah," I said. "But listen, do you think we can get together before then? I need to talk to you."

"Sure, if you don't mind having every breathless word recorded."

I'd forgotten that the rest of the band was being followed by MTV. And every second of what they recorded was on our Web site. Each of our pictures was featured on the main page of the site, so I clicked on "Julian" and—just like that—there he was. Driving his '65 Falcon on a two laner that passed through open farmland on the outskirts of Twin Oaks. Talking to me.

I have to say, Julian looked as good as I remembered. I found that comforting. *Something* hadn't changed, anyway.

"That could be a problem," I said, referring to having every breathless word recorded. "This is kind of private."

"I don't think I can shake these guys." Julian looked at someone in the backseat. The camera panned to reveal a familiar-looking busty blonde who was more than happy to return Julian's smile. I think her name was Shania. One-name Shania. I'd seen her on MTV hosting one of their shows.

"If you're watching, Regina, there's no way I'm letting Julian out of my sight!" Shania bleated into the camera.

"You hear that?" Julian asked.

"I'd have to be deaf not to. Listen, we'll talk after the concert."

"OK. See ya." Julian snapped his phone shut before I had a chance to say good-bye. I continued to watch him on the computer as he pointed out some local landmarks for Shania. Then I exited our Web site and frowned.

First, Dad. All uptight about something. Now Julian. Playing it cool with me. That definitely wasn't my imagination.

My frustration suddenly turned to anger. Why on earth had this weird Fairy Godmother of mine given me no memory of anything leading up to this particular day? That was downright cruel.

As I looked around at the ton of Caverns merchandise that

surrounded me, I had the strange sensation that this was not so much a wish come true as it was some kind of maze that I could get increasingly lost in.

Music has been my sanctuary for as long as I can remember. Playing it. Listening to it. And the Cavern is where I play my music. The Cavern is the basement rec room of my house. It has a dingy gray concrete floor and concrete block walls painted white. Not much to look at, but it's the heart and soul of the house as far as I'm concerned. For those of you who are not Beatles nerds, my basement—and my band—are named after the underground club in Liverpool where the Beatles played before they were famous.

So the Cavern is where I retreated after talking to Julian. I needed to play my guitar, lose myself in my music, and just forget about everything for a while. But as soon as I walked down the steps to the Cavern, it was obvious that I couldn't get away from my new life. The Beatles posters that had hung on the walls—the inserts from *The White Album*, a *Help!* movie poster—were gone and had been replaced by, natch, Caverns posters and pictures.

The pictures were quite informative, actually. The Caverns had apparently played everywhere from New York to London to Paris to Rome. We had met—and been the opening act for—Coldplay and Kings of Leon and Belle and Sebastian, to name a few.

Too bad I couldn't remember any of that!

As I turned slowly in the middle of the room and stared at all of those pictures, I heard a phone ring upstairs. Dad came down to the basement with my cell phone. He didn't look too happy as he handed it to me.

"It's Bradley," he said.

Bradley? Who was Bradley? "Hello?" I answered warily.

"Regina!" a strange voice yelled.

Dad hovered nearby. He looked like he wanted to stick around to monitor the conversation. But he finally turned and went back up the stairs.

"Yeah?" I responded when he was gone.

"Everything OK? I couldn't get you on your Web site. What's up?"

"I'm just not feeling too good, that's all." I was going through the motions of the conversation but trying to figure out if I knew a Bradley from school, or somewhere else.

"You're still coming to L.A., though, right?"

"Of course."

"What time's your arrival?"

"I . . . don't know."

"That's my girl. Listen, give me a call when you get in. I'll be on set so you might have to leave a message."

On set? Where was this guy calling from? Suddenly, a picture in the corner of the room that I hadn't noticed caught my attention. As I walked toward it, I said, "I will do that."

"You sound weird, Regina. Sure you're OK?"

"It's been a crazy day," I replied.

"Crazy day? Try a crazy year! No wonder you're feeling a little whacked out. But I'm here for you, baby."

The picture showed me with my arms around a gorgeous hunk of a guy. It took me a moment to place him. When I did,

I felt faint. Just like I had upstairs. Really, I went all light-headed and my cheeks got hot and I had to sit down.

"You still there?" the voice asked. I decided to try out my theory of who I was talking to.

"Yeah, I'm still here. How's everything on *P.C.H.*?"

"Same old, same old. We're at the beach today."

Bingo. My theory was correct. I was talking to *Bradley Sawyer.*

A quick word about Mr. Sawyer.

He's one of the stars of *P.C.H.* (aka *Pacific Coast Highway*). For those of you who haven't seen it, *P.C.H.* is a hybrid of *The O.C., The Hills, Gossip Girl*, etc., etc. Young and restless teen-agers cavorting in Malibu, California, as they juggle high school, dysfunctional families, the opposite sex, and budding acting careers.

To be honest, I'd only seen the show a few times. But Brad-ley's face had been plastered on the covers of all the teen mags for the past couple years or so. ("The new Brad Pitt!" one teen mag had anointed him.) He was definitely one of the current teen gods.

"Listen, babe, they're calling me to makeup. Can't wait to see you."

"Me, too," I replied. I don't know why I said that, but it just seemed like I should.

"Can't get you out of my mind, girl. Hey, just to tease you a bit . . . I've got something special planned when you get here."

"Really? What?"

"If I told you, it wouldn't be a surprise, would it? *Bye.*"

Bradley sent a little kissing sound my way, then signed off. I sat like a statue, phone still plastered to my ear after Bradley had hung up. Of all the surreal, mind-blowing things that had slapped me in the face since I got up just a few hours before, this one actually took the cake. I mean, how does one deal with something like this?

I mentally rewound the conversation I'd just had. Judging from the evidence:

I had met Bradley Sawyer at some point in my travels and was now dating him.

He expected me to call him when I got to L.A.

He had a special surprise lined up for me when I got there.

As I sat thinking about all of this (farther into the maze?), I decided there was only one thing to do at that moment in time. Store all of this new info in the Later Department of my brain. (Unfortunately, a lot of things languish there.)

Then I went upstairs to get something to eat.

8

I have been known to eat prodigious amounts of strangely grouped foodstuffs when I'm stressed out. A pregnant woman would have nothing on me when I really get going.

So there I was, not long after having a big breakfast, sitting at my dining-room table and chowing down on ice cream, processed lunch meat, olives, and some kind of dried fruit when Dad came into the room and sat down across from me.

"What on earth are you eating?" he asked with a frown.

I looked at the various dishes in front of me and replied, "Stuff."

Dad shook his head in dismay, then slid a folder across the table to me.

"Trey e-mailed your itinerary for the week. I just printed it out."

Trey? Who was he?

I turned the folder around and opened it. Inside was a neatly typed list of what the Caverns would be doing during our week in L.A. It included:

Staying at a place called the Sheraton on the Strip
A final recording session at Capitol Records for our new CD
Shooting a video for "He Loves You"
Playing on the *Tonight Show*
Rehearsal for the Grammys the day before the ceremony
Finally, the Grammys

"Doesn't leave a lot of time for Mom, does it?"

That stopped me cold. I was going to see Mom? She hadn't been a part of my life for over five years. After leaving us all those years ago, she'd moved to California and had started a completely new life. She'd called me maybe a half dozen times in all those years.

"No, it doesn't," I said. My anger and bitterness about my mom leaving always seemed to be just below the surface of my everyday emotions. Always lurking there, waiting to come up and bite me.

"You don't have to see her if you don't want," Dad said. I got the impression he wouldn't mind if I didn't.

"I'm going to," I said. "I'm definitely going to see her."

Dad nodded. "Please be careful of Trey, OK? I don't trust him. Matter of fact, I really think you need to find a new manager."

So that's who Trey was. My manager. That answered one question, at least. But there were still too many mysteries. Way too many mysteries.

Dad got up to leave, then said, "By the way, Regina, don't think you can get out of our agreement. You definitely haven't been living up to your end of it." I didn't know what Dad was talking about, so I tried to look properly apologetic and said, "I'm sorry."

"Sorry doesn't cut it. I'm telling you right now, if you don't have all of your assignments done the week after we return from the Grammys, that's it. You go back to school. And I'll go right back with you. If I can get my old teaching job back, that is."

OK, another little mystery solved. My dad and I had both left T.J., and I was being homeschooled. And flunking out, from the sounds of it. At least that seemed like an easy problem to deal with. "I promise I'll have all of my assignments done the week after I get back."

"I'm holding you to that promise, Regina. I don't care if you have your album to finish. Or a tour to plan. None of that matters to me. I told you from the start you have to keep up with your education if you're going to do this."

I nodded contritely.

"OK, enough of that. We'll be leaving for the concert before you know it. I know how long it takes you to figure out what to wear. Better get to it."

Dad stood up and left the room. I stayed for moment, staring at the itinerary. My week in L.A. was suddenly feeling like an epic journey of some sort. At least I had the T.J. concert for a warm-up. Yes, at least I had that before heading off to Oz.

When I opened my closet door, I was so blown away I almost toppled over. Timberrrrrrrrr! I'm not kidding. I mean, the clothes! You couldn't believe the clothes. It was the most prodigious collection of funky and beautiful threads I had ever laid eyes on.

There were gorgeous jackets, tutus in every color imaginable, T-shirts from around the world, dozens of jeans, vintage bell-bottoms, '60s pegged-leg pants, skirts of all shapes and lengths.

And the shoes! I don't know where to start with those. But the ones that immediately caught my eye was a classic pair of Beatles boots.

Black leather. Cuban heeled. Zipped to just above the ankle. They were famous the second the Fab Four put them on, back in the '60s. But in this wacky new world of mine, the Fab Four never had worn them. Maybe I did. Maybe they were my trademark. Maybe *I'd* made them famous!

It took me several hours to try on all of those clothes. I felt like Cinderella, preparing to go to a rock 'n' roll ball. For the first time since I'd woken up and been confronted by my strange new world, my what's-happening-here? expression had been replaced by a grin. Which was good. Girls need to have a little fun. Once in a while, anyway.

When Dad yelled from downstairs that we were leaving in ten minutes, I had finally decided on my outfit. It was an official black T.J. T-shirt, with T.J. on the back in large gold letters. Over the T-shirt, I wore a black bolero jacket with really beautiful, intricate gold embroidery. (I knew the crowd would love it when I took off the jacket at some point in the concert to show off the school letters.) A black tutu, black stockings, and of course, the black Beatle boots finished things off.

I have to say, I thought I looked pretty good. Which is saying something, because I'm usually extremely critical of my entire . . . persona.

"Regina! You ready?!"

Looking at myself in the mirror, I nodded. I was as ready as I was gonna be. Then, from out of the blue, I did something that surprised me.

I clicked my heels three times.

Why did I do that?

Even now, I really can't say. Maybe because I'd thought of L.A. as Oz just a little while earlier. Or maybe I wanted, subconsciously, to return to my normal, ordinary world.

One thing's for sure. Nothing happened when I clicked my heels. I was still in my room. The Regina Bloomsbury doll still stared at me from her perch on the shelf. I still felt like I was on the wildest roller-coaster ride of my life. At that point, I was just hanging on for dear life. And wondering where this fairy-tale roller-coaster ride was going to end up.

9

I could see the lights from miles away. Hollywood lights is what I call them. The kind that shoot a single beam into the air so high that it touches the clouds. There were four or five of them. I couldn't be sure exactly how many because they were moving around in a crazy kind of white-light dance in the dark night.

My stomach started its own kind of dance when I saw those lights. They made everything seem very real somehow. But unreal at the same time, if that makes any sense. They were like some kind of cosmic exclamation point to the fact that I was about to play a concert for my T.J. peers. The very ones who barely knew I existed just the day before.

Weird.

I looked at Dad as we approached the driveway that led to the school. He looked really cool. He was dressed in black jeans and a black turtleneck and a black sport coat. His hair was kind of spiked out. I hadn't told him that I thought he looked cool, so I did just then.

"Thanks, honey. Glad you think so. I wanted to be somewhat

presentable. It's not every day a dad gets to be onstage with his famous daughter."

Onstage?

Was Dad playing with the Caverns? Or maybe he was just introducing us. Whichever, I would find out soon enough. When Dad turned into the T.J. driveway, there were two cop cars blocking the way. Just beyond them were several MTV vans and a large crowd. One of the policemen approached us and asked for IDs. Only students and teachers were allowed to attend the concert, he explained. But then he noticed who I was and said, "*Miss Bloomsbury*. No need to show your ID." And he waved us on by. Dad gave me a raised-eyebrow expression as he drove past the police cars with their serious-looking rotating red lights.

The Hollywood lights were set up right in front of the school. A huge crowd milled about, steam bursting from their mouths in the cold night air. Everyone stared at our car as it moved past. Then someone yelled, "It's Regina!" and the chase was on. I felt like I was in a scene from *A Hard Day's Night* as several dozen people broke away from the crowd and ran after our car, which Dad drove around the side of the school to the auditorium door at the rear.

The irony was not lost on me when I realized that the concert was being held in the auditorium. It was the same place where I had approached Mrs. Densby to ask if the Caverns could play at the Back to School dance. And been turned down. Now the Caverns were playing there "live" to a worldwide audience!

When I got out of the car, I was swamped by my pursuers. Mostly younger girls. They shoved CDs and pictures at me to sign as Dad tried to make a path to the auditorium door. I was intimidated by all the worshipful attention, to be honest. It felt really strange.

"*Let her through!*" a voice boomed menacingly from the open auditorium doorway. An outdoor overhead light illuminated, in dramatic fashion, a stout figure.

It was good old Mrs. Densby. She was the Gold General that evening. "There will be a signing session after the concert! It was announced to the entire school after final period!"

My admirers reluctantly shrunk away from Mrs. Densby, mumbling insults under their breath. The Gold General followed their departure with a frown. But her demeanor changed instantly as Dad and I approached the door.

"Regina," she purred. "Come right this way. We have everything set up for you."

The next hour leading up to the concert was a blur. I had trouble focusing. I felt hot one moment, cold the next. It reminded me of the time when I was in sixth grade and had to give a speech in front of the entire middle school on Presidents' Day. Only this was a bit bigger than that.

The hour started out with Mrs. Densby leading me and Dad to the dressing room backstage. My bandmates were already there, having done a sound check earlier. With the MTV cameras hovering uncomfortably close, recording and broadcasting all this for our live Web cast, Julian and Lorna gave me cool nods when I entered the room.

Lorna was especially standoffish. "Nice of you to join us," she said, giving me a critical up-and-down as she checked out what I was wearing. It looked like fame hadn't altered Lorna's pissy attitude, that's for sure. But I was determined not to let her infect me with any doubts about the outfit I had chosen. This was *my* wish come true, after all.

"You have the set list, Regina?" Danny asked. Stationed next to the table with all of the food, he could have been a poster boy for the proverbial kid in the candy store.

The set list! I hadn't even thought about that. "I'm . . . working on it," I said. Lorna rolled her eyes. Which was captured by one of the cameras. Whatever issues were going on between us, I'd have to figure out later. First things first.

I asked Dad for a piece of paper and pen, exited the dressing room, found the girls' lavatory and locked myself in a stall. My hand was shaking as I wrote "Set List" at the top.

That's as far as I got. I sat on the toilet and stared at the blank piece of paper. Without warning, the weight of the last twelve hours came crashing down on my shoulders. I wasn't strong enough for all of this unexpected fame. I wasn't ready for it. I felt like I was going to crumble. Breakdown Time. Catatonic Girl.

I heard the lavatory door open, then Julian saying, "Don't even think about following me in here!" to the gaggle of MTV people following him. There was the click of the door lock, then footsteps moving toward me. A knock on my stall door.

"Is this a private moment?" Julian asked. I literally started to sweat. What was Julian doing here?

I tried to compose myself, then slowly opened the door. If Julian hadn't been acting so cool toward me earlier, I would have rushed right into his arms. He looked so great, for one thing. He was dressed all in black. Black jean jacket. A faded black T-shirt with THE CAVERNS painted on it, the paint cracked from too many washings. (He had painted T-shirts like that for all of us, in my basement, shortly after the band got together.) Then there were the black pegged-leg jeans and beat-up boots that only Julian could wear so well.

"So . . . spill," Julian said.

"What?" I asked, feigning ignorance.

"C'mon, Regina. You sounded really uptight earlier when you called. Matter of fact, you're acting pretty weird right now. What's going on?"

"This set list," I said lamely.

"No way is it the set list." Julian gave me a curious look. "But let's start with that." Julian hopped up on one of the sinks and turned it into a chair. "What do you say we do something different for a change. Open with 'Yesterday.' A nice slow song. Which means the audience will have all this pent-up energy, see? So when we hit 'em with 'He Loves You,' it's gonna knock 'em right out'a their seats."

I liked that idea, so I wrote down those two songs. "Great. What next?"

Julian took a moment before answering. "I think we should do another song from *Meet the Caverns!* 'Eight Days a Week' maybe, then introduce one from our next CD. Just to tease 'em, you know?"

"The next CD?"

I must have looked a bit perplexed and concerned when Julian mentioned the next CD, because he gave me another curious look.

"The next CD! Of course! Sure!" I said this way too enthusiastically, so I concentrated on my set list to avoid Julian's suspicious scrutiny. After adding "Eight Days a Week" to the list, I asked, as casually as possible, "Which song do you think we should do?" That's what had thrown me off when Julian suggested that we play a song from our next CD. The Caverns Web site hadn't listed any of the songs, so I didn't have a clue what to put down.

When I looked up, I was relieved to see that Julian's expression had softened a bit. "Is that what's freakin' you out, Regina? Are you worried about how people are going to react to our next CD? The sophomore slump and all that?"

That sounded like as good a reason as any to explain my odd behavior, so I nodded yes. Julian smiled. "Allow me to ease your anxious brow, OK? The songs on *Something New* are every bit as good as the ones on our first CD. Some of them maybe even better. When *SN* comes out? I guarantee it's gonna cement your place as one of the best songwriters we've seen in a very long time."

The way Julian said that last sentence . . . I thought maybe he was jealous of me or, rather, jealous of my supposedly great songwriting talent. Maybe that's why he was acting all stand-offish. Julian was a pretty good songwriter, after all. We played a couple of his songs in the Caverns. Well, the other Caverns. The Caverns that existed in the *real* world.

Whether or not that was true—the jealousy thing—Julian hid it pretty well as we filled in the rest of the song list, which included "If I Needed Someone" and "Drive My Car" from our second CD. Then he totally surprised me when he slid off the sink and extended a hand toward me. "What do you say, Regina? Let's take it to 'em. For old times' sake."

Old times' sake? I wasn't sure what that meant, but I'm telling you, when Julian reached out his hand, it felt like the prince asking for a dance.

As I took Julian's hand, his touch sent a ripple of electricity through my fingers, up my arm, and all the way to my hot head. Julian gave me a slight, somewhat rueful smile, then we walked out of the girls' room, hand in hand.

10

"Ladies and gentlemen . . ."

A roar exploded from the crowd on the other side of the curtain. Standing in the middle of a dark stage, my knees started to rattle. I'm not kidding. It felt like my legs had been plugged into a socket or something.

"Live from Twin Oaks's Thomas Jefferson High . . ."

A bigger roar. I desperately tried to will my knees to stop shaking.

"Streamed to the United States and beyond . . ."

Now the roar was nonstop. And the shakes had spread to my arms. It dawned on me—really for the first time—that this concert had the potential to be a total disaster.

"The Caverns!"

No turning back now, however. The curtain opened, a spotlight hit me like a slap, and the roar of the crowd enveloped me like a wave, the kind that knocked me off my feet at Atlantic City when I was a kid and drove me headfirst into the sandy ocean floor. Which I kind of liked, actually.

But this—this aural assault—was stunning. It was *Cavernmania*. The cheering was so loud in the auditorium, I couldn't hear myself play. I was way too nervous to make eye contact with the crowd, so I kept my eyes locked on my acoustic guitar as my trembling hand strummed the musical introduction to "Yesterday."

This is what you wished for, I reminded myself as I waited for the crowd to settle down. *Don't blow it!*

When a hush finally fell over the auditorium and I croaked out, "Yesterday," the famous first word of one of the most famous songs ever written, another roar rocked the place.

As it turned out, Julian's idea of doing "Yesterday" first was a brilliant stroke. After the craziness of the day, what I really needed was to be still. I needed to focus.

Ironically, it was in front of hundreds of people that I was finally able to do that. Not at first, though. I was more than a bit shaky at first. I sang some truly prodigious off-key notes, which didn't help my trembling extremities. I desperately ad-libbed a musical bridge between the first and second verses to buy some time and try to calm myself.

It didn't help matters that Lorna was staring at me in dismay about five yards away during my freak-out time. But it was Lorna's glare that actually gave me a kick in the butt to move on and try to do justice to one of the Beatles' most beautiful songs. I wasn't about to let *her* bring me down, that's for sure.

Don't blow it.

So I started singing the second verse. Still a bit tentative in my delivery, but feeling a little better. It definitely helped when I heard the strings—those gorgeous strings—come in behind me.

Wait. What? Strings?

Glancing to the side of the stage, I saw my dad playing the synthesizer, making the instrument sound exactly like a string section. I'd been so totally out of it in the final minutes leading up to the concert that it hadn't even registered on my frazzled brain that he was going to be playing the song with me. Tucked away on the side of the stage, barely visible—Dad was never one to hog the limelight, as opposed to Mom—he glanced up and gave me an encouraging smile.

That should have helped, having Dad onstage with me, but it made me nervous all over again. I didn't want to blow it with him right there, and the both of us on computer screens all around the world. So I just tried to hold it together and get through the song, when suddenly an incredible thing happened.

All of my anxiety and trembling *simply slipped away*! I kid you not. It was totally amazing. In an instant, I had inexplicably entered a zone. It was . . . well, it was as though I were playing "Yesterday" for the first time. Discovering it for the first time. Bringing something new and fresh and real to it.

In short, I lost myself in the music. Truthfully, it felt to me as though something outside of myself—my Fairy Godmother, perhaps?—was looking over me and helped get me into that zone. If that was the case, I'd take it. But really, Fairy Godmother or not, what I experienced during "Yesterday" was that magical feeling that comes along very, very seldom.

Like a first kiss. Or an unexpected compliment. Or having one of those rare days when everything just seems to go right for a change. Point being, when you taste any of those things, you're hooked. You definitely want to taste them again.

When I got to the end of "Yesterday," I wanted to taste it again. The feeling I had when I played the song. All I wanted to do was play another song and another and another and never stop. It was like I was under a spell or something.

Which maybe I was.

The final chord of "Yesterday" hung in a quiet auditorium like an invisible bridge between me and the audience. Then the crowd leaped up and roared. I stood on the stage, all alone in the spotlight, a big smile on my face. Then I gave my dad a little bow of thanks—the spotlight quickly going to him for a couple of seconds, which was cool—but after returning the bow, Dad immediately retreated backstage, and the spotlight was back on me, bright and blinding.

It was a transporting moment, that's for sure. I didn't want the beautiful vibe to dissipate even the slightest, so I quickly exchanged my acoustic for my Strat and counted out the beat for "He Loves You." Danny kicked in with the short, snappy drum intro and the Caverns were off and running. The crowd didn't sit down for the rest of the set.

How could they?

"I Want to Hold Your Hand," "Please Please Me," "We Can Work It Out," and "Help!"

One great, irresistible song after the other. Which the band played with incredible force, tightness, and skill. I was shocked at how good we were. But then, we had been traveling the world doing this for quite a while now.

Again, weird.

But I didn't dwell on any of that during the concert. Any of what had happened *before* that evening. I just played my heart out. And had the time of my young life. I couldn't believe how comfortable I felt after the first song. It was as if I had been born to be onstage.

I bounced all over the place, sometimes singing harmony with Lorna, sometimes with Julian, mimicking the way Paul and George or John and George would sing together at the same mic. I've always loved seeing them do that, for some reason, on the concert DVDs I have.

I had such a good time that I was disappointed when we came to the last song. But then I reminded myself . . . there's more of this to come! The band launched into the final song, which was the Beatles' terrific version of "Twist and Shout," and the students were suddenly going wild and twisting in the aisles, and teachers and security guards tried to shoo them back to their seats, but that didn't work, and then some of the kids surged toward the stage, and a couple of them hopped up onstage and started twisting next to me and then dove back into the crowd when the guards came after them.

We kept playing right through all the terrific turmoil. After hitting the exuberant last chord of "Twist and Shout," we did our Beatles Bow, then the curtain closed, and we left the crowd cheering and begging for more.

As we left the stage, Danny and Lorna and Julian and I cracked up when we heard Mrs. Densby's voice blare over the sound system that such behavior would not be tolerated. She would "shut it down" if everyone didn't calm themselves. Which would mean no signing session!

We grinned at each other, sweaty and happy, and knew we had rocked the place something special. It was a terrific moment. Whatever was going on behind the scenes, between me and Julian and Lorna and Danny, didn't matter just then. We were a band at that moment. We were one. And as far as wishes went, this one felt like it had kicked in.

Big-time.

11

The signing session was allowed to proceed, in spite of the fact that Mrs. Densby had her hands full controlling the still-boisterous crowd. Students were lined up in front of the signing table, laughing and jostling, as some of the younger ones broke from the line to chase one another around the auditorium while waiting to say hello to their hometown heroes.

As the Gold General tried to corral the disruptive students like a frustrated cowhand, the band signed everything from T-shirts to posters to dolls to special vinyl editions of *Meet the Caverns!* Even girls in my class who had never given me the time of day shoved Caverns merchandise in my face and gushed about how great the concert was.

Then a girl who looked like she was eleven or twelve handed me a photo album. Inside was the entire history of the band, told in press clippings and articles from not just the teen mags and *Rolling Stone* but also *Time* and *Newsweek* and even *The New Yorker.*

I hadn't noticed anything like this at home. So I got totally caught up looking through the album until the girl gave me a little cough to remind me that she was there. I asked her what her name was.

"Joelle," she replied.

"I have a big favor to ask, Joelle." Joelle's eyes expanded in surprise. A favor? What kind of favor could Regina Bloomsbury possibly ask of her?

"This is the most incredible collection of articles on the Caverns I've ever seen," I explained.

"I like you guys a lot," Joelle replied, pleased with my compliment.

"In that case, do you think you could let me keep this for the next week or so? I'll write something very special in it and deliver it to your house. Myself."

There were two responses at war in Joelle's eyes. She was hesitant to let go of her precious album. But she was definitely excited as well. Regina Bloomsbury, coming to her house?

"We'll have a photo session when I get there."

That did it. Any concern Joelle had about parting with her painstakingly put-together album disappeared in an instant.

"It's a deal," she said, sounding remarkably grown up and businesslike all of a sudden. "My address is on the inside cover."

"OK," I said, and gave her a smile.

"By the way," Joelle said as she turned to go. "I hope you don't mind me telling you this . . ."

"Of course not. What?"

Joelle leaned close toward me and spoke in a whisper. "I love Bradley and all, but I still think you and Julian were great together. Sorry, but that's just how I feel."

You could have pushed me over with your pinky finger at

that moment. Julian and I had been together in this wish world of mine? As Joelle walked away, I was aware of Lorna shooting me a curious look.

I tried to compose myself. It wasn't easy, after what I'd just heard. But I managed to give Lorna an innocent shrug and—indicating Joelle's album—said, "I haven't kept one of these. Have you?"

12

"Glorious Rock 'n' Roll!"
"The Caverns! The Return of Innocence!"
"Bloomsbury: The Suburban High Priestess of Pop!"

Those were just a few of the headlines in the various articles in Joelle's album. But I wasn't interested in all the rave reviews of *Meet the Caverns!* I needed the behind-the-scenes stuff. The stuff about me and Julian.

First I had to deal with Dad, though. After we got back from T.J., he clearly wanted to sit for a spell, have a cup of coffee, and talk about the concert. He was proud of me, I could tell. Besides that, I think he was pretty pumped about the fact that he had just played for a worldwide audience—in addition to "Yesterday," he accompanied us on "In My Life" and "Drive My Car"—even though he wouldn't admit that.

But almost as soon as we sat down, calls from L.A. and New York started coming in. The MTV people were ecstatic about the early estimates of how many people had streamed the concert, which was, like, a lot. Trey couldn't wait to tell us about the requests he was already getting from concert promoters in obscure places around the world, desperate to get us on our next worldwide tour.

Then Mom called.

Dad spoke to her very briefly—and tersely, his good mood instantly vanishing—then handed the phone over to me.

"Hi, Mom," I said tentatively.

"My god, what a fantastic concert!" Mom wailed. She sounded just like one of the T.J. teens who had lined up for autographs. She really did. "You were brilliant, Regina! Absolutely brilliant!"

"Thanks, Mom." It felt so weird to be talking to her. Surreal is what it felt like.

"I can't wait to see you in L.A.," Mom practically yelled over the phone. It occurred to me that she and I had probably seen each other sometime over the past year. At least Mom had seen *me*.

"You know what, Mom? We have to get up really early tomorrow. I better go." I surprised myself, saying that; I just couldn't deal with a phone conversation with my errant but suddenly very attentive mom at that moment.

"You blowing me off, Regina? Is that what you're doing? Blowing off your mother?"

"No. It's just—"

"I'm kidding! Go get your beauty sleep. Just wanted to call to tell you how terrific you were."

"Dad was pretty good, too, don't you think?"

Mom didn't answer right away. Then she said, "I guess, but you were the star, honey!"

Very confusing. I mean, now that I was famous, here Mom was, calling and saying how great I was? It gave me kind of a bad feeling, to be honest. But my reaction to hearing Mom's voice for the first time in ages was actually more complicated than that. No matter how much she might have put me off with her gushing, I found myself desperately wanting to believe that if I went back to being just Regina . . .

Mom would feel the same way about me.

"Well, good night," I said.

"Night, Regina. I'm staying at the same hotel as you. Did your dad tell you?"

Did he? I couldn't remember. "Ah . . . yeah," I lied.

"See you in La-la Land, honey!"

"Bye." I hung up and just stood there in the kitchen for a moment. Even at this hour, I could see a few paparazzi outside, bundled up in heavy snow jackets to ward off the cold, hoping to get a shot of me through the windows.

Weirdness, weirdness, and more weirdness.

I said good night to Dad at that point, then—feeling kind of spacey and hungover from my brief conversation with Mom—went upstairs and got ready for bed.

Finally, I would be able to look through Joelle's album. I curled up with the bedside light on and started to go through it. First, page by page, but then I got restless and jumped ahead to see if there were any pictures of me and Julian.

There were plenty of pictures of me, that's for sure. It was disorienting and very strange to see so many photos of myself. (I don't like to have my picture taken.) There were pics of me with the band. On the red carpet at the MTV Video Music

Awards, People's Choice Awards, Teen Choice Awards, Nickelodeon Kids' Choice Awards. With celebs like Taylor Swift, Eminem, and Rihanna. Then, with a flip of the page . . .

Bingo.

My heart did a flip-flop when I came across the *Teen People* photo of Julian and me kissing. *Kissing!* The accompanying article chronicled a day at the beach Julian and I had spent together on an off day during our U.S. tour, which—judging from the date on the corner of the page—had been about six months before.

Other photos, captured by a telephoto lens, showed Julian and me strolling hand in hand in the sand. Me kicking water at Julian from the surf. Our kissing photo was the last one of the bunch.

I have to tell you, this, more than anything, made my current amnesia especially cruel. I had kissed Julian. And had no idea how that felt!

There were a few more pictures that documented our relationship, and I felt worse seeing each one. There was one of me holding on to Julian's shirttail as we perused an outdoor bookstall in London. Another that showed us singing together during a concert, our faces intimately close. But the photo that really got to me was us having coffee at a sidewalk café with the Eiffel Tower in the background.

We'd been in Paris together!

I stared at that picture for quite a while. A familiar sensation boiled up inside me as I looked at Julian's face, smiling at me across the small circular table on the sidewalk of that Paris café.

Anger at my Fairy Godmother.

I got up, went to my computer, and turned it on. But then I realized that I didn't have any idea how to get in touch with my F.G. Why? Because she didn't tell me, that's why! I went to my Gmail account and angrily typed out an e-mail.

Why did you just throw me into this? Without any preparation? Without any memory? I thought Fairy Godmothers were supposed to help their princesses!

I addressed the e-mail to fairygodmother@gmail.com and sent it. Of course I didn't expect a response. I just needed to vent a little. As I sat staring at the computer, something slowly dawned on me. Maybe I was truly on my own at this point. It could be that my wish had been granted and that was that. From here on, it was up to me to work things out. I reluctantly turned off the computer and trudged back to bed. The photo album, which I had tossed aside when I went to the computer, had fallen open to yet another picture of me.

But this one was of me and Bradley Sawyer.

There we were, smiling at each other on the set of *P.C.H.* The photo accompanied an article that explained why I was on the set of one of the most popular shows on television. "We Can Work It Out" had been on the show's sound track, to much success, so a meeting had been arranged for me to stop by and say hello to the cast.

I stared at the photo, transfixed. I mean, *the way Bradley was looking at me.* It was absolutely bizarre to see myself being devoured by someone's eyes like that. Nobody had ever looked at me like that before. Remotely.

So it was with some wariness that I flipped through the

rest of the album, which filled in some of the blanks of my "relationship" with Bradley. The pictures showed the two of us hanging out in L.A. and—yes—there was a kissing photo of us as well. I'd become a kissing fool and didn't even know it.

The really bad thing I discovered in one of the mags was that I had apparently broken up with Julian after meeting Bradley. I couldn't believe it. Why would I do such a thing? At least now I knew what Julian had meant when he said, "For old times' sake."

As I looked at one photo after another of me and Bradley, I got to thinking, what kind of person *am* I in my new world? I mean, I simply couldn't imagine leaving Julian for this bronzed, megawatt-smile Adonis. OK, I can hear you thinking, *What are you complaining about? He sounds gorgeous!*

He is, definitely. And considering that I had nobody and no prospects just the day before I made my wish . . .

But here's the thing. It was pretty much impossible for me to picture myself in Bradley's world. It was too . . . exotic, if you know what I mean.

On the other hand, I'd be lying if I didn't admit to feeling a little tingle of excitement seeing myself in that world. With Bradley. Wouldn't any girl want to experience that? Even if just for a little while?

Bling!

Startled to hear the familiar sound of my computer, I looked up to see that it had turned on all by itself! I slid off my bed, walked slowly to my desk, and watched as these words appeared on the screen:

Sorry, Regina. I meant to get back to you earlier, but this is an especially busy time of year for me. I did manage to get to the concert, however. Yes, that was me helping you over the hump. But you did the rest. Great job!

P.S. I forgot to mention something earlier before I had to scoot. (I'm so spacey sometimes!) If you have any further questions, log on to wish-come-true.uni. Gotta go! See you in L.A.!

When the words on the screen disappeared in a puff of smoke—that's exactly what it looked like—I sat down, logged on to the Net, typed "wish-come-true.uni," and hit the RETURN key.

Sure enough, a Wish-Come-True Web site quickly appeared. (Imagine, the Web has become so much a part of our lives that I didn't think twice about a Fairy Godmother having her own Web site!) Before I could go any further, however, I was asked by a computer-like voice to give the name of my first pet.

I had to think about that one. I had a turtle when I was around eight, named Clarissa, so I typed that into the blinking box.

GOOD ANSWER ! ! ! !

. . . flashed on the screen, and the plain-looking graphics dissolved into what appeared to be a live shot of a beautiful castle high in a snowy mountain setting, with a peaceful, crystal clear stream gurgling in the foreground. Very fairy tale–like. Words started to scroll up from the bottom of the screen. They read:

> **Hello, Regina. First of all, welcome! Second of all, know this about your wish-come-true world. *It's anything you want it to be.***
>
> **If you just want to have a good time, it can be that.**
>
> **If you want to learn a few life lessons, it can be that as well.**
>
> **Or you can treat it like a game, where everything you do is like a move on a game board, which has consequences.**
>
> **Not all that different from real life, when you think about it. Life, after all, is what you make of it. But your wish-come-true world is very different from real life in one very important way.**
>
> **You have six days to decide if you want to stay in this world. For you, Regina, that would be the Grammys. Once you accept an award (Inside scoop: You'll win more than one!), that's it. You're in this world forever.**
>
> **So have a great week! (And who knows, maybe beyond . . .)**

When the final line disappeared at the top of the screen, the image of the castle remained. And the mesmerizing sound of that gurgling stream.

Several thoughts bounced around in my brain after reading the scroll of words. For starters, it was about time my Fairy Godmother had given me a clue about what was going on. God, she really was spacey!

But I did feel a bit better about this new world of mine. It was just a game. At least that's how I was suddenly looking at it. Of course I wasn't going to stay in my wish-come-true world. That would be cheating, right?

As far as the cheating part went, everything had been going so lightning fast since I got up in the morning that I hadn't really given much thought to the fact that I was bogus famous. Famous on someone else's songs. I hadn't wished for the Beatles to disappear, however, so it wasn't really my fault. Even still, a guilty kind of feeling had been lurking behind all the frenzied activity. Jabbing at me, you might say.

But this solved everything! Now I could go to L.A. with a clear conscience, have a great time, then come on back home to my real world. No harm, no foul.

But aaaaaahhh . . . nothing is ever that easy, that clear-cut, is it? That's one of the things I was about to learn in L.A., anyway. Yes, folks, as I finally drifted off to sleep that night with visions of a Cinderella-like L.A. journey dancing in my head, little did I know that I would gradually morph into an altogether different fairy-tale figure.

That would be Pandora.

Just like that fabled character, I was about to open the pro-verbial box. . . .

And discover what was inside.

PART
L.A.
TWO

1

Sunny Cal.
Land of Make-Believe.
Tinseltown.
Hollyweird.

I've heard L.A. called many names, but it all added up to one thing. *The unknown.* It was a mythical land to me. I could only imagine what it was going to be like, being there.

Think about it. The surf culture. The Strip. The Dream Factory. L.A. was where all those wonderfully campy beach-party movies had been made. Where *P.C.H.* was currently being made. And to think I was about to land right smack-dab in the middle of it!

But as our plane approached the West Coast, L.A. was still very much a mystery to me. I couldn't see it, is why. A solid layer of clouds between the plane and the ground below obliterated even a glimpse of the place.

Then, as a stewardess told us to be sure that our seat belts were fastened and our seats were in the upright position and all items were stored under the seat in front of us, we began our descent.

And suddenly, we were inside the clouds. I was staring at pure white. It was as though we'd arrived in heaven or something. It was a lovely, peaceful feeling, actually. The calm before the storm and all that.

Then, as if we'd fallen through a hole in that heaven, everything cleared and . . .

There it was!

It didn't register at first. My first thought when I saw L.A. below me was, *Could it really be that big?* Not big in an up kind of way but in an across kind of way. You really have to see it to believe it. The buildings and houses *go on forever*. They stretch as far as the eye can see.

"Everything cool?" Julian asked. I had the window seat. Julian was next me. We were in first class, mind you. That had taken some getting used to, but it was clear to me when we boarded the plane that Dad and Julian and Lorna and Danny were used to all of this from our worldwide travels and kind of jaded about it. So I had to try to pretend it wasn't the first time I'd been on a plane in first class.

I hadn't been able to mask my surprise at the sight of L.A., however, and Julian had just witnessed my wide-eyed wonder.

"Yeah, I'm fine," I said, trying to affect a slow, sleepy, seen-it-all-before drawl. "Why?"

"You just looked kind of . . . surprised or something. Almost like you've never seen L.A. before."

"What? *No.* But you know . . . everytime I see it . . . it makes Twin Oaks look like a backwater town."

"That's because it is," Julian said, then he went back to his book. Unfortunately, he had resumed his cool attitude toward me after the concert. At least now I knew why. It was me who broke up with him, after all.

When I looked around the first-class section, I saw that Lorna was asleep, Danny was flirting with a stewardess, and Dad was studying something in a loose-leaf folder.

OK, Regina, I thought as the foreign buildings of L.A. rushed up into clearer focus. *This is it! Get ready for . . .*

Recording sessions!

Video shoots!

The *Tonight Show*!

In short . . .

Rock 'n' roll fantasy dreamtime!

But as I tried to pump myself up for what promised to be an outta-sight week of nonstop excitement, I felt uneasy. I knew why. How could I truly enjoy myself while constantly surrounded by my surly bandmates?

Maybe it was all part of the game. Something I had to work out.

OK. I would. But first things first. Namely, settling into the Sheraton on the Strip, my new home away from home. As I pictured what it would look like . . .

BAM! SCREEECH!!!

Yelps of surprise erupted throughout the plane. The pilot immediately brought the massive hunk of metal under control after the bumpy landing and taxied it toward the distant terminal.

Quite a wake-up call. I took a deep breath and exhaled slowly. It might have been a rude welcome, but at least we had officially arrived in the Land of Make-Believe.

...

Giddy. Disoriented. Already kind of time-laggy. I felt all of those things when we got off the plane and headed for the baggage claim area. Somebody by the name of Abernathy met us there. Everyone looked happy to see him. When he gave me a smile of greeting, I tried to act the part of someone who knew who he was.

But when Abernathy led us out to the sidewalk and put our baggage into the back of *a mile-long white Hummer limo*, I laughed out loud. Everyone stopped in their tracks and stared at me. After an awkward moment of silence, I explained, "I just can't get used to this." Then I quickly hopped into the limo to escape the curious looks and slid along the plush white leather seats that lined both sides of the amazingly long interior.

Lorna gave me one of her laserlike glares as she settled into her seat across from me. She was definitely the most suspicious of my behavior. I got the impression Lorna was going to do whatever she could to find out what was wrong with me.

All just part of the game.

I tried to act like a jaded rock star to deflect even more scrutiny from the person who was shaping up to be my Wicked Witch of the East in this fantasy world of mine. So instead of eyeballing the brand-new-to-me urban landscape as Abernathy drove us to our hotel, I grabbed a magazine from the rack next to my seat and tried to focus on the first article I opened it up to.

Wouldn't you know it. There was a picture of me and Bradley Sawyer.

The Sheraton on the Strip is located, where else, on the famous Sunset Strip. As we zeroed in on our hotel, I allowed myself a peek from behind my magazine to check out the ginormous billboards that lined the street. The four-story-tall movie and rock stars smiled down, godlike, on us little people below.

Suddenly, there *we* were. I can't even begin to describe the feeling when I saw us. It was just so totally out there and unexpected. The billboard was the *Meet the Caverns!* album cover, only a million times bigger. It hovered over the Strip, right across from the Sheraton, as it turned out.

When we got out of the limo, I looked up at our half-shadowed, nonsmiling faces. We looked like ancient sphinxes or something. Inscrutable. Not giving anything away. But cool. Definitely cool.

"I know. You can't get used to that, either. Right?" Lorna said this with dripping sarcasm as she brushed past me and walked into the hotel. A group of paparazzi were snapping away nearby. They would have been right on top of us but were prevented from getting any closer by a long cordon and a couple of security guards. Julian raised his eyebrows at this latest barb from Lorna, then grabbed his backpack from the trunk.

As I watched Julian walk in that cool way of his toward the hotel—the paparazzi documenting his every step—the word *confidant* resurfaced in my brain. I knew it could be very difficult getting through the week without one. And much less fun.

So, yeah, a confidant. Someone I could talk to. Someone who could fill me in on the behind-the-scenes drama of Caverns

Land. Dad didn't fit that description. I'm sure Mom wouldn't. Or my Fairy Godmother, from the looks of things. So that left Julian.

But how could I talk to him about all this without his thinking I had totally lost it? That was something I had to figure out. And the sooner, the better.

The paparazzi were calling out to me to look their way as a porter arrived to get my luggage. I gave them a quick, shy smile, then—before following the porter into the hotel—I gazed up once again at that amazing Caverns billboard.

Well, Regina, I thought, *you're not in Twin Oaks anymore. That's one thing for sure!*

2

Turns out we had tickets (practically impossible to get, apparently) for the House of Blues our first night in L.A. The Black Eyed Peas were playing a benefit for Rock the Music! and the place was going to be packed with the cream of the crop from the music biz.

"Trey says it's a great photo op for the band," Dad told us as we dined in the hotel restaurant on the top floor. Mentioning Trey, Dad's voice definitely had an edge to it. The restaurant was practically deserted. At four o'clock, it was early for dinner, but not for us. Our stomachs were still on East Coast time.

"I think I'm gonna pass on tonight, if it's OK with you, Mister B." Everyone looked at Julian, surprised. "I want to get settled in and ready for the week," he explained.

"Me, too," I said, immediately realizing this could be the perfect opportunity to talk to Julian. In response to everyone's stares, I added, "I'm still not feeling quite right."

"OK," Dad said. "Lorna? Danny?"

"I'm goin'!" Danny exclaimed. "Sure you don't want to come, Regina? Sounds like a blast!"

"It does, Danny. But I think I need some downtime."

Danny shrugged and gave me his happy nod. But then he frowned, and I got the impression he was wondering whether or not I was telling him the truth about why I wasn't going to the House of Blues.

As for Lorna, she said, cool as can be, "I'm in."

Dad handed tickets to Lorna and Danny. "Show starts at eight."

I was aware of Lorna giving me another one of her suspicious looks as I polished off my zuppa di pesce, which was really good soup, I have to say. Not to knock my dad's—and sometimes my—cooking, but I'd never had anything like this at home, that's for sure. Matter of fact, I'd never even heard of zuppa di pesce before that night at the Sheraton.

We were finishing up our dinners when Dad said, "By the way, I got word that Chris Rock is going to be guest host when you play the *Tonight Show*."

"Cool!" Danny replied.

"Yeah, I thought you might like that. He's doing the Grammys as well, so it'll be good. You'll already be pals by the time you get to the Shrine."

I was excited to hear about Chris Rock. Besides the fact that he's one of the funniest guys around, I love *Everybody Hates Chris*, and the thought of meeting him was . . . actually, it was just too weird for me to even process. Like the huge billboard of the Caverns outside our hotel, meeting someone like Chris Rock was yet another thing that made my L.A. trip feel surreal, as if it weren't actually happening.

The surreal moments kept coming when I got back to my

room after dinner. The light on my phone was blinking, so I sat cross-legged on my bed to figure out what numbers to hit to get my message.

"Hi, babe! We're filming late tonight, so unless you want to stop by the set, we'll have to get together tomorrow. Give me a call!"

I smiled and shook my head when I heard Bradley's voice. He sounded like a lively one. But no way could I deal with Bradley at that point. Like a lot of things in my new life, he would have to wait. As I went to take a well-needed shower, there was a knock on the door. It was Dad.

"Just wanted to stop by to see how you're feeling," he explained after I opened the door.

"I'll be all right. Wasn't sure if I could take an exciting evening my first night in L.A., that's all."

"I hear you."

"Want to come in?"

"That's OK. I'm going to crash." Dad gave my room a quick once-over. "Room's acceptable?"

"More than."

"Listen, I also wanted to let you know your mom called. She'll be here on Friday."

Let's see, that was in . . . three days. Good. Another thing I could deal with later. I gave my dad a nod.

"OK," he said. "Night." He gave me a hug, then as he went off down the hall, "Remember, recording session ten a.m. tomorrow."

Suddenly a young girl came barreling around the far corner and charged in my direction. Two security guards were right behind her. When she saw me, she yelled, "Regina!" The guards caught up with her before she got to my door. Dad barely acknowledged the struggling tweener as he passed her by. This was something he was more than used to.

"I just want your autograph!" the girl wailed. "I already got Julian's!"

The girls who had been yelling outside my house and the ones who had jumped all over me outside the T.J. auditorium had been kind of faceless to me. But here I was, one-on-one with a wide-eyed fan, and I felt a sudden surge of affection for her. She looked so vulnerable. So young. Actually, she looked kind of like me when I was her age.

"Ummmm, excuse me? Officers?" I said this as the guards were leading the girl away. They stopped and looked at me, still holding her firmly by the arms. "All she wants is an autograph." The girl's anguished expression was swept away by a huge smile of relief and triumph.

"OK," the taller of the two guards said reluctantly.

The excitable girl, whose name was Emma, kept up a constant stream of chatter as I signed her vinyl copy of *Meet the Caverns!* "I-love-you-guys-I-can't-wait-for-your-next-CD-but-you're-my-real-inspiration-Regina-I-want-to-be-a-singer-songwriter-just-like-you."

Waving good-bye to Emma as the guards led the now-passive girl down the hall, I heard her words echo in my head. *I-want-to-be-a-singer-songwriter-just-like-you.*

Yeah, I thought, watching Emma disappear behind the closing elevator doors at the end of the hall, *I guess I do, too.*

3

Julian was playing a song on his guitar as I approached his room. I had never heard the song before, so I stood at his door and listened. I wanted to hear it all the way through.

The song was upbeat, with a catchy chorus. It was good. Julian hummed along, which led me to believe he didn't have lyrics yet. So that's what Julian wanted to do instead of going to the Black Eyed Peas concert. Work on some original material. When the music stopped, I knocked on the door.

Julian looked genuinely surprised to see me. Maybe it was what I wore. I had changed into baggy pajama bottoms and a tank top.

"To what do I owe this honor?" Julian asked coolly.

Tired of his attitude, I said, "Cut it out," and pushed past him and went into his room.

"For all you know, I might have had someone in here with me," Julian said provocatively. That hadn't occurred to me for some reason. "The place is swarming with fans, after all."

"I know. I ran into one." I took Julian's guitar, sat on his bed, and strummed it. "I was listening outside your door. I like your song. New?"

"Yeah. Well, I've been working on it for a while."

"No lyrics?"

"Not yet."

"Maybe I could help you."

"That's OK." Julian said that fast and firm.

"Why not? We've worked on songs together before."

I tensed after I said that. Julian and I had worked on a couple of songs together in my pre-wish world, but had we done that in this world?

"That was a long time ago, Regina."

Whew. One slipup averted. I stayed put on Julian's bed, working my way tentatively through his song, trying to remember the chords.

"Why are you doing this?" Julian asked, a hard edge to his voice.

"What? All I asked is if I could help with your song."

"You know what I'm talking about. Coming here in your PJs. All familiar-like. What's going on? Why aren't you with Bradley?"

Good question, I suppose, from Julian's POV. I put his guitar down gently, then walked to the balcony. Like my room, it overlooked the Strip. The House of Blues was right across the road. The place looked like it was built from hundreds of pieces of discarded wood and sheet metal and had exploded on the spot right there on Sunset Boulevard. It looked like an elegant scrap heap.

My eyes wandered from the House of Blues to my and Julian's and Lorna's and Danny's gigantic faces. They stared at me from the billboard, which was almost level with Julian's tenth-floor balcony.

Julian followed me outside. We both stood, silent, leaning against the railing and breathing in the scent of the night air. Down below, traffic moved restlessly along the Strip. Horns honked. People yelled and talked loudly as they waited to get into the House of Blues.

In contrast to the noisy energy below were the mute, endless lights of L.A., which were visible from our tenth-floor vantage point. Like a gently twinkling carpet, the lights softly illuminated the night in all directions. Except on the horizon to the right of where we stood. There the lights ended abruptly.

"So that's the . . . Pacific Ocean over there, right?" I asked. "Where the lights suddenly stop?"

"Well, yeah," Julian replied, as though it was common knowledge.

The Pacific was like a blank in the night. A large, mysterious expanse of black lurking beyond the lights of L.A. It was sort of like the unknown pressing up against the known. Rubbing shoulders with it, so to speak.

"Julian, do you believe in alternate universes?" That's what my strange, hyperdrive wish-come-true world felt like to me all of a sudden. As in, while I was experiencing this new life, I was still trudging through my normal life at the same time. In some other time zone altogether.

"Never really thought about it," Julian replied.

"Do you think it's possible, though?"

Julian didn't answer right away. Which was normal for him. Whenever you asked Julian a question, he tended to think about it first. Looked at it from all angles, you might say. He did that now, then said, "I think we're such a speck in the grand scheme of things that I have a hard time getting all that excited about the big game on Friday nights." I couldn't help but smile. The answer was so Julian.

"I have amnesia."

Whoa! That just popped out. I was as surprised as Julian when I said it. I hadn't come to Julian's room with any kind of game plan, after all. Hadn't worked out what I was going to say. I guess my subconscious decided to take over. Whatever, it was out there now. Too late to turn back.

"Come again?" Julian looked skeptical, to say the least.

"Yesterday? When I wasn't feeling so good? Before I called you? I went down to the Cavern to play some music." I was riffing, of course. Improvising like a madgirl. "I fell down the steps and hit my head."

"You're kidding me."

"No."

"And, what . . . you have amnesia now?"

"Yeah."

"What can't you remember?"

"Anything! I mean, this morning? When you said it looked like I was seeing L.A. for the first time? It *was* the first time! I can't remember being here before. Last night? When it looked like I was freaked out before the concert? I *was* freaked out! I can't remember any of the concerts we've played in the past year!"

Julian gave me an under-the-eyebrows kind of look. He was sizing me up. Trying to figure out if I was goofin' on him.

"I don't remember us being together. I don't remember us breaking up. I don't remember meeting Bradley. I don't remember *anything* since around the time we recorded our first album."

I said all that in a rush, desperately wanting to convince Julian that I was for real.

"If you don't remember us being together, Regina, how did you even know to say that just now?"

"From a scrapbook a girl gave me at the concert last night. That and our Web site is my only source of info."

Julian stood on the balcony for what seemed an eternity, looking at me. *This isn't working!* I thought. *What am I gonna do now?*

But then the lights from the Strip, reflecting in Julian's eyes, showed a very subtle change in his blue-green irises. He believed me. I could tell. Relief!

"This is very weird, Regina."

"*Tell* me about it!" I exclaimed, following that with a strange little hiccup of a laugh.

"You need to see a doctor. Right away." I could see the concern in Julian's eyes. That made me feel pretty good.

"I know. But not this week, Julian. I can't be going to doctors and shrinks or whoever you see when your mind's gone blank on you. This is such a special week, you know?"

Julian took a breath, then exhaled slowly. He leaned on the railing and looked off down the Strip with a frown. "Why are you telling me about this? Why not your dad?"

"Dad'd take me back to Twin Oaks *tonight* if I told him. No ifs, ands, or buts." Julian nodded. He knew that's exactly what my dad would do. "I promise I'll tell Dad as soon as we get back home next week."

"So what do you need from me? Besides sympathy?" Julian actually smiled at that moment. It was great to see that smile again.

"I don't know what's going on, Julian. I know we're in L.A. for the Grammys, of course. I got that from our Web site. But for starters, I don't know why everyone's so ticked off at me. You, I figure it's because we broke up. But all this tension. It's terrible. What's goin' on?"

Julian turned suddenly and went back inside. What was he doing? I followed him to find out. Julian sat in the stuffed chair in front of the TV and indicated the sofa next to the chair. "Have a sofa, Regina." I jumped over the back of it and sat cross-legged at the end near Julian.

"Why's everyone so ticked off at you?" he asked. I nodded. "For one thing, rumor has it that after our tour this year to promote the new album, Trey wants you to go solo."

"Get out. Seriously?"

Julian nodded. "Let's face it, we're basically backup musicians to you at this point, but we're making a lot more money than backup musicians. If you cut Lorna, Danny, and me loose, all Trey has to do is pay a one-time fee to studio musicians for your future recordings. That way you—and of course *he*—stand to make a lot more money."

"No way would I kick you all out of the band." I was offended Julian would even consider such a thing.

"Ahhh, but rumor also has it that you're seriously considering staying here in L.A. after the Grammys. There's really no reason for you to be in Twin Oaks anymore. It'd be a lot easier for you to go solo after our tour if you've already moved to L.A., right? Wouldn't even have to look us in the eye to tell us we've been cut."

I was stunned to silence, hearing this. It wasn't what I was expecting, that's for sure. But it was just a warm-up to what came next.

"Other than that, you've been a bit of a pain in the ass for quite a while now."

"What? I have? How?"

"Lording over the recording sessions. The video shoots. Being a diva, basically."

"I'm not like that," I protested. "I can't imagine ever being like that."

"Neither could I. At first. But when everyone tells you how great you are, every day, over and over, I guess a person can change."

I stared blankly at the TV, which was playing some nature show. A lion was roaring at some of the "little people" of the jungle, letting them know who was boss.

"Anything else you want to know?" Julian asked.

There were lots of things, but I didn't feel like getting into them just then. It was enough to learn about my diva-ness and possibly staying in L.A. and going solo. When I looked at Julian, a suspicious frown creased the area between his eyebrows.

"What?" I asked.

"You said that you can't remember anything since we recorded our first CD."

"Around that time, yeah."

"So you don't remember recording any of the songs for our second CD?"

I tensed up, sensing a trap coming, but my brain felt all jumbled, and I couldn't think straight enough to figure out what it might be. "Rrrright."

"I know you wrote all the songs for *Something New* after we recorded the first CD. Which means you can't remember writing them, right? So how did you manage to sing those two new songs last night? You coulda listened to our first CD for the old stuff before you came to the concert, if you needed to brush up on them. But the new material . . . you didn't know we were gonna play those songs until I suggested it. And yet you didn't flub one line."

Oh, no, I thought. *He's got me there.*

"Well . . . ," I said, my mind racing, frantically searching for an acceptable explanation. After quickly discarding several, I grabbed one and went with it. "I guess music gets in your head so deep it's hard to forget."

My reply struck me as being somehow lame and profound at the same time. I hoped Julian would buy the "profound" part.

"OK, Regina," he said, looking at me kind of sideways with one eye slightly closed, an expression he used from time to time to signal wariness. Or thoughtfulness. "I'll do what I can to help you this week. But then you have to go see a doctor."

"Deal."

4

As I padded back to my room, I felt much better about things. For one thing, I had seen the return of Julian's smile. That was worth a ton, believe me. For another, my brief confab with Julian explained a lot.

My bandmates were angry and uptight because they thought I was going to leave them behind in the dust. That, plus my diva-like attitude. But, really, me . . . a diva? I still couldn't believe it.

As for Dad, he was concerned that I wasn't going back to Twin Oaks with him at the end of the week. Which would leave him all alone at 489 Lynn Drive.

Both issues were easy to deal with. I would simply announce, before our recording session the following morning, that I did not intend to leave the band or stay in L.A.

Tensions eased.

Everyone relaxed.

A fun week is had by all.

I smiled and nodded to myself as I continued down the deserted hall. Passing the elevator, I was aware of the doors opening and a couple emerging into the hall. I casually glanced at them . . . then quickly looked away.

That's Fergie and will.i.am! I thought feverishly, my heart pounding at my first celebrity sighting since arriving in L.A. I knew I shouldn't look back at them. After all, *I* was an international celebrity. Which meant I should be all cool-like, right? Still, I wasn't Fergie or will.i.am.

So I couldn't help but take another look over my shoulder. The two superstars were walking off down the hall, talking. I almost called out to them to have a good concert—it was too early for them to have played at the House of Blues—but I held back. It was exciting enough just to see them up close like that.

I shook my head at the wonder of it all. Then I grinned like a little kid. *This is more like it. Definitely what a wish come true should feel like!*

After my sudden celebrity sighting, which had come right after my encouraging talk with Julian, I was *so* much more optimistic about the coming week. Arriving back at my room, I slid my key card through the slot. . . .

And screamed.

Actually, I'm getting ahead of myself. First, I opened the door. Then, I went into my room. Then, I fell backward onto my bed. *Then*, I screamed. And immediately sat up on the edge of the bed as my eyes zeroed in on a nearby stuffed chair.

That's because Bradley was lounging on it! "Hi, babe," he said casually. "Scare you?"

My mind felt strangely independent from the rest of me as it furiously tried to arrange a group of words into something resembling a reply. Not an easy thing to do under the circumstances, but still I was kind of disappointed with what my mind came up with.

"How . . . how'd you get into my room?"

Bradley held out his hands in a way that said, *How do you think? I'm Bradley Sawyer!* Then he stretched his arms high over his head, stood up from his chair, and cracked his neck with a quick back-and-forth movement of his head. "Had to do a ton of surfing on set today. Muscles are kinda stiff." I nodded, but didn't know what to say in return. But I sure knew what I was thinking.

My god, what a good-looking man!

Pictures simply didn't do him justice. As he headed toward me, *Adonis* was the name that popped into my head. I'm serious. The blond hair. The chiseled chin. The way he moved, so assured and confident. As I thought of gods and the rest of us mortals, Bradley sat down next to me, gave me a warm smile, and leaned in for a kiss.

"No!" I shouted, leaping from the bed.

Bradley looked at me like I was nuts. "What's wrong?"

Good question, actually. Who wouldn't want to be kissed by this guy?

"I, ah . . . I might still be contagious," I explained.

Bradley slid across the bed and got up on the other side in an attempt to put as much distance as possible between us.

"Thanks, Regina. Very considerate."

"Yeah, the last thing I want to do is get you sick."

"Especially with the scene I have to do with Melissa tomorrow."

"What . . . you've got . . ."

"A big beach-kissing scene."

"Tough job," I said, feeling strangely jealous.

"Somebody's gotta do it." Bradley gave me another one of his dazzling smiles. It was a smile to melt a girl right into her stocking slippers. His perfect teeth seemed to sparkle, like in one of those commercials where they digitally apply a twinkly gleam at the edge of a tooth.

"So we'll just have to . . . kiss another time," I said.

Would we? I wondered, already kind of regretting my retreat from Bradley's attempted smooch. It had been such a shock, though, finding him in my room. Besides, I didn't even know this guy! Which is why I had jumped up from the bed like that, of course. However, having had a few moments to get my bearings, I must admit I felt like I was already falling under the spell of Bradley Sawyer.

"OK. Rain check," Bradley said. "You do look kind of tired, Regina."

"I am. Sorry you came all this way."

Bradley frowned. "I could jog here from my house if I wanted."

"Oh, yeah. Right." *Store that info*, I thought. *You've been to Bradley's house and apparently it's pretty close by.*

"You *are* out of it, aren't you, girl?"

"Yeah. Between being sick and the time change and the Grammys. I'm flummoxed. That's what I am. Flummoxed."

Bradley gave me another megawatt smile. "That's what I love about you, Regina."

"What?" I asked, genuinely curious.

"You're still so . . . Twin Oaks." Bradley walked around me to the door. He was hesitant to even get near me, so I held out my elbow, the way Gene Wilder did to Madeline Kahn in *Young Frankenstein*. (One of my favorite movies. You should see it if you never have.) Bradley didn't get what I was doing. I guess he wasn't familiar with the movie. But then he figured it out, reached out his bent arm toward me and we touched elbows.

"Come by the set tomorrow? We're filming at night."

"To watch you kiss Melissa?"

"It's only a TV world, Gina. This is real life." For Bradley, I guess it was. He opened the door, then froze. Staring at the doorknob he had just touched, Bradley took a bottle of hand sanitizer from his jeans pocket and cleaned his hands.

"Good idea," I said. "Better to be safe than sorry. Especially with that kissing scene tomorrow."

Bradley smiled as he walked backward down the hall. Just before getting on the elevator, he blew me a kiss. I caught it and held it. I was still holding it when the doors of the elevator closed and Bradley disappeared from sight. I went back into my room and stood by the bed, thinking about what had just happened.

What an absolutely bizarre experience, I thought. *For one thing . . . when had I become so irresistible?*

The obvious answer? Since I had become famous.

Famous.

It was actually starting to sink in. I was famous. And for the rest of the week, I would be famous. And irresistible. And talented.

At that point, one week seemed like plenty of time to enjoy my wish come true. At that point, seven little words had not yet surfaced in my brain. But they were about to, with increasing regularity as the days to my departure from this world of wonders ticked by.

What seven little words? you may ask.

"A girl could get used to this."

5

Capitol Records.

If there is such a thing as a church in the music business, the famous round Capitol Records building in Hollywood, California, would be one.

I tried not to show my awe when we arrived in the lobby the following morning. But the framed gold and platinum records that plastered the walls of the reception area were enough to get my heart galloping like a scared little filly.

Frank Sinatra. Judy Garland. The Beach Boys. Pink Floyd. David Bowie. Queen. The Foo Fighters. Radiohead. And . . .

The Caverns!

The sight of our platinum album hanging on the wall with all of those musical greats calmed me down a bit. *See, you belong here!* Well, not really. But I reminded myself to just enjoy the experience. This was all a lark, after all.

When we got to the first-floor recording studio, I looked around the room. Plain-looking. Nothing fancy. But the vibes. Just thinking about the giants who had recorded here made me feel giddy and *alive*.

Meanwhile, this was nothing new to Julian and Lorna and Danny. Julian and Lorna tuned their guitars as Danny snapped off paradiddles on a rubber pad that covered the snare drum. They looked very professional, my bandmates did. They fit right in.

I caught Julian glancing at me from the corner of his eye. He looked curious about how I was dealing with all this. Considering my amnesia. I shrugged. He raised his eyebrows, nodded, then went back to his tuning.

"Hi, gang!"

A young man in his thirties or thereabouts entered the studio. He had a Starbucks cup in his hand and an intense look in his eye.

"Hey, Trey," Danny called to him from across the room.

So this was Trey. He had "the look," I'll say that for him. Black goatee. Buzz cut hairstyle. Expensive-looking California casual clothes. Confident as a rooster. Julian gave Trey a nod as he walked past him toward me. Lorna ignored him.

"Ready to lay down some more magic?" Trey asked when he arrived at my side. I felt uncomfortable with how close Trey was to me.

"Yes," I said.

"Good. Let's get started." Then in a lower, confidential voice, "Then we can call this baby done and get on with your new life, girl."

That stopped me cold. I had planned to announce to everyone that I wasn't going solo. Wasn't staying in L.A. But Trey had this *thing* about him. He had . . . presence. He radiated power.

So, OK, tell your bandmates and Dad later, I consoled myself. *What's the difference? So long as you do it.*

Trey had joined Dad and several other people in the control booth. Hands on hips, he stood at the large window overlooking the studio. He looked like he was surveying his property or something.

That made me kind of uneasy, so I concentrated on tuning my guitar. Julian had given me a heads-up on two things before we got to Capitol. One, we always rocked out with a few of our old songs before each recording session. Two, we were recording "Rain."

I was delighted to hear that "Rain" was going to be the last song we were recording for our *Something New* CD. It's one of my absolute favorite Beatles songs.

So after we wailed on "He Loves You" and "Help!" and were all warmed up and relaxed, the producer, who had a long braided ponytail that snaked down his back, said over the loudspeakers, "OK, let's run through 'Rain' a couple times."

And that's when the trouble began.

"Rain" has a great and very distinctive Paul McCartney bass part. Especially on the last chorus, where he goes into a triple-time tempo against the four-time beat. I'm not sure if that describes it very well, but you'd know what I mean if you listened to it. Anyway, I knew Paul's bass line. Lorna didn't.

So I had to grit my teeth and tried to ignore the fact that Lorna was playing it all wrong the first time we went through the song. And the second time. Danny wasn't playing the drums exactly right, either. There was a real war going on in my head, let me tell you. Two voices, jawing at each other.

Let it go, said one.

I can't, said the other.

Voice One: *What's it matter?*

Voice Two: *This is the Beatles we're talking about!*

Voice One: *So what?! This is just for fun!*

Voice Two: *But they're doing it all wrong!*

When the producer said, "Let's do a take," my Beatles voice won out. *Just be nice about it, Regina.*

"One second, please," I said very nicely.

The room immediately went silent, and everyone gave me an uh-oh kind of look. Lorna glared at me. That gave me pause, but I pushed on.

"The thing is, I have a few ideas for the bass and drums."

"No. You don't," Lorna immediately countered.

OK. All righty, then. It looked like I was going to have a fight on my hands. So what to do? All eyes were on me. It was my move.

I thought things through before responding to Lorna's challenge. I really did. But my final thought was, *This is my wish come true. Not Lorna's. If I can't please everyone this week, I should at least please myself.*

"Yes. I do have some ideas, Lorna." I said this as calmly as possible, but I could feel my eyes narrowing as the words came out.

Lorna just glared at me. I stared back. It was a glaring-staring contest between the two of us. Predictably, Danny avoided any kind of eye contact.

"Lorna, I think you should listen to what Regina has to say." This came from Trey in the control booth.

"Of course you do," Lorna shot back. "She's your prize. Your number-one gal."

"It's her song," Trey said evenly. "She wrote it. She should be able to express her opinion on how it should be played."

"Then she can play the bass part herself." Lorna unplugged her guitar, put it in the case, and strode out of the studio. I watched Dad, who was still in the control booth, go after her. Being a teacher, he was really good at dealing with volatile teen behavior. I had a feeling he wouldn't be too successful dealing with Lorna.

OK, I thought. *That went well.*

6

"I can't help it. I hear the songs in my head. Every part. Everything."

We'd finished our morning recording session, which did not see the return of Lorna. Turns out we didn't need her. I handled the bass part just fine. As for Danny, he was definitely ticked off at me for instructing him how and where to put in more drum rolls, but at least he listened to me.

Julian and I were at a huge two-level music store called Amoeba. There were tons of used CDs, vinyl records, and 45s. The walls were plastered with posters of every band imaginable, from Jimi Hendrix to the Ramones to U2 to the Caverns to the Instigators.

The Instigators?

Anyway, every band except for, of course, the Beatles.

"You're a genius, Regina," Julian said matter-of-factly. He was leafing through the Oasis albums. "And you're always right. That bass part you played? Perfect. Your idea to loop the final chorus in reverse? Who would have thought of that? But now you see why you have the diva label. That's what you've been doing all along. Telling everyone how to play their parts."

I absentmindedly leafed through some albums as I listened to Julian. *Let it go*, I told myself. *Don't try to defend yourself. You did the right thing.*

Suddenly, I came across a Monkees album. "This isn't right," I said. "If the Beatles don't exist, the Monkees shouldn't."

"What?" Julian asked.

"Oh . . . nothing. Just talking to myself."

Julian pushed the Oasis albums back into place and headed down the aisle. I followed him. I wanted to ask him something. Something I had been curious about. "Julian?"

"Mmhmm."

"When you first heard my songs. What did you think?"

"What did I think?"

"Yeah, I don't remember how you reacted."

"I was blown away. I couldn't believe what I was hearing."

"Did you believe that I wrote all of them?"

Julian looked over his shoulder at me. "What's that supposed to mean?"

"No hidden meaning."

"Of course, I thought you wrote them all. Why wouldn't I?"

"Well, I never played any of them for you. Then, all of a sudden . . . what . . . how many songs were there?"

"A dozen. Maybe more."

"And that didn't seem kind of strange? All at once, *bam!*"

"I was surprised you hadn't played any of them for me before. They were all great. But I think your dad is right."

"My dad? What did he say?"

· 113 ·

"He thought writing those songs was your way of dealing with the pain of your mom leaving. But you weren't ready to let them out . . . to let anyone hear them. Then, for whatever reason, you let 'em fly."

Mom.

Julian mentioning Mom brought that familiar, complicated feeling rushing to the surface. I still couldn't believe I'd be seeing her in a few days. I had not a clue what that would be like. *Later,* I told myself. *You'll deal with that later.*

"You know what? I gotta go." Julian was looking at a clock near the line of checkout counters.

"You gotta go?" I repeated, surprised. Julian hadn't mentioned anything about going anywhere.

"Yeah. I'll take a cab."

Abernathy was waiting for us outside.

"Where you goin'?"

"Just . . . somewhere." Julian looked uncomfortable as he strode toward the exit.

"Somewhere? You mean, like, a girl kinda somewhere?" I already knew the answer to that one. I could smell it. I could. Julian gave off a scent.

"Yeah, like a girl kinda somewhere." Julian said that as though he were talking to a juvenile. "You wouldn't know about Hayley, Regina. She and I haven't been in the teen rags."

I flashed hot when Julian said that. It was obviously meant to be a crack about all the media attention Bradley and I had received.

"So, what . . . is this Hayley like a girl-in-every-port kinda thing?"

Ouch. What a terrible thing to say. And I regretted it the second I said it. (Note to self: Try to edit some of your thoughts before saying them!) I could see Julian's ears literally turn red.

"Yeah, that's me, all right. I'm a girl-in-every-port kinda guy." Which Julian definitely wasn't.

We were out on the sidewalk by this point and Julian looked up and down the street for a taxi. "You know, Regina, I'm actually glad that we broke up. Band relationships never work. Better to just be friends."

"Is that what we are? Friends? Doesn't feel like it right now." What it felt like was . . . Julian abandoning me.

"What do you want me to do? Babysit you?" Julian held his arm up for the lone taxi traveling down Santa Monica Boulevard.

"Oh, real nice, Julian. Real nice."

"Hey, don't try to make me out like the bad guy. I wasn't the one who broke this up!" Julian swirled his finger in the space between us, indicating the two of us as a couple.

"I thought you just said it was good that we broke up!"

"It was! It is!" The taxi stopped on the other side of the street from where we were.

"So what are you complaining about? After all, it didn't take you much time to find someone else!"

"Oh, give me break, Regina."

"No, *you* give *me* a break!"

We were starting to sound like two little kids having an argument on a playground. Julian shot me an exasperated look, then ran across the street to the taxi.

"Have a good time with *Hayley*!" My parting shot.

"Say hi to *Bradley* for me!" Julian's.

I watched Julian hop into the taxi. Then I spun on my heel and went off in a huff to look for Abernathy.

7

I felt like a caged animal when I got back to my room. Pacing, back and forth, back and forth, as one question pounded at the inside of my skull.

What happened?!

My first full day in L.A. and I had managed to alienate Lorna and Danny and—to top things off—got into a fight with the one person I could talk to in this new world of mine. My confidant!

Calm down, Regina! It's not the end of the world! I took deep breaths and tried to ease my heart rate down from the BOOM! BOOM! BOOM! stratosphere.

The hot tub! That's it! Take a nice, long soak! That'll make you feel better! I knew I had to do something to calm myself down. 'Cause at that point, I was even thinking in exclamation points!!!

I was on my way to the bathroom to fill up the tub when I noticed the message light blinking on my phone. It was a Bradley message, wanting to know if I was coming to Paradise Cove in Malibu, where they were filming.

Of course! Bradley! Why hadn't I thought of calling him?

He was exactly what I needed after my tension-filled day. A sympathetic ear.

Instantly forgetting about the Jacuzzi soak, I went on a tear to figure out what to wear. Bradley had seen me in my old PJs and tank top. Time to look a bit better than that.

OK. They were filming a beach scene in Malibu. So what does one wear to a beach scene in Malibu on a February night? I hadn't bothered to unpack since arriving in L.A., so by the time I answered that question, my three suitcases looked like they'd exploded and spewed clothes and accessories all over the place.

My outfit for my Malibu excursion? Old, faded jeans, a long-sleeved tee with AN OLD-FASHIONED GIRL printed on the front, my red Converse sneakers, and a bright red hooded sweatshirt with a pouch in the front.

Red seemed like a good choice. It signaled . . . I don't know, everything from "Danger" to "Excitement" to "I'm out to have a good time!"

Anything I wanted it to be.

It was good that I was trying to have a bit of fun at this point in my journey. Because the really intense stuff was just around the corner.

"Can you take me to Malibu tonight?"

Abernathy, who apparently was our round-the-clock driver, was sitting in a chair in the lobby of the Sheraton, reading *Rolling Stone*, when I approached him. He hesitated for a moment, then said, "It would be my pleasure, Miss Bloomsbury." When I told him we were going to the *P.C.H.* set at a place called Paradise Cove, he seemed pleased.

"Have you ever seen that show, Abernathy?" I asked as he held open the door of the limo for me.

"Never miss it."

"Terrific. Maybe you could fill me in on the story line on the way." I felt like I should know something about the show, seeing as Bradley probably figured I watched it all the time.

"I'm surprised you don't watch your own boyfriend's show, Miss Bloomsbury," Abernathy said—kind of echoing my thoughts—as he negotiated the ridiculously long Hummer into the stream of traffic on Sunset. He had put down the window between the driver's seat and the back of the limo, and I sat as close to the front as I could so we could talk.

"Please, Abernathy. Call me Regina."

"Will do, Regina. Anyway, it's good we have some time before we get to Paradise Cove. 'Cause there's lots been goin' on, on *P.C.H.*, let me tell you."

"I'm all ears," I replied, and settled in for the ride.

By the time Abernathy was driving, appropriately enough, along the Pacific Coast Highway, I was hopelessly confused. "Wait a second," I said, interrupting Abernathy's revelation that Sean was in love with Lindsay. "I thought you said that Sean was in love with Janie."

"He was. But not anymore."

"But Janie's still in love with Sean?"

"Always and forever."

"OK," I said. But not very convincingly.

"Complicated, I know." Abernathy smiled from the front seat. "But let's cut to the chase here. The main thing you need to remember is that Zane doesn't really love Stephanie." Zane was the character played by Bradley.

"Right, right. He's just dating her because her father is a big-shot producer."

"Exactly. He'll use anyone he has to, to get where he wants."

"He's such a bad boy."

"Juiciest part on the show, though. Everyone loves a good villain, after all."

I nodded, then settled back in my leather seat and looked out the window at the beautiful scenery. I couldn't believe I was actually in Malibu. To get to the place, we had to drive through a range of mountains. The sun had been low on the horizon when Abernathy steered the Hummer along the twists and turns of the mountain road, making the hills glow with all kinds of colors. It felt like we were leaving the ordinary world behind and entering a fabled land, going through that mountain pass.

"That's Cher's house," Abernathy said, pointing out a palace-like mansion with a wall around it that was perched on a high bluff overlooking the ocean. "At least I think it's still hers. It's hard to keep track sometimes." Reflecting the rosy colors of a beautiful sunset on the ocean horizon, the house looked absolutely radiant. It looked like the queen's palace in this fairy-tale land.

Can you believe this, Regina? I suddenly asked myself. *Can you believe what's happening to you?*

At that point, I really couldn't. It was still just too unreal. I felt like if I blinked, it would all go away. Not long after Cher's house sighting Abernathy turned left off the PCH and onto a narrow side road. As he drove past a sign that read PARADISE COVE, I thought . . .

Don't blink, Regina.

8

A film set is a surreal kind of place. Especially at night. After giving a security guard my name, Abernathy was waved past a ticket booth at the bottom of the road. There was a restaurant just to our left. Beyond the restaurant was the beach.

Banks of bright lights were set up on the beach. A nearby pier was outlined in Christmas-like white lights, which were reflected in the water flowing past the pier. The whole scene looked like an amusement park, without the rides.

After Abernathy parked the limo, he opened the door for me and said, "I'll wait for you here."

"Thanks, Abernathy. And thanks for the rundown on *P.C.H.*"

"My pleasure."

I gave Abernathy a smile, then headed toward the bright lights. The closer I got to them, the faster my heart beat. This was exciting, after all. I'd never been on a film set before. Well, actually, I was, once, when my parents and I went to Orlando and Disney World for a vacation. But it was hot and I was cranky and nothing much was going on.

But at Paradise Cove, plenty was happening. A cluster of people were near the lights and camera and a large fire burned in a nearby pit. Beautiful swimsuited boys and girls sat around the fire. Someone played a guitar. More gorgeous gals and guys played volley ball near the fire pit, their bods bouncing and well-oiled skin flashing in the firelight. All of this activity seemed to be in service of a scene that was being rehearsed near the camera as I approached.

"Can I help you?"

The person who came up behind me couldn't have been much more than twenty years old. He wore a headphone, a jacket to ward off the chill evening breeze, and carried an official-looking notebook. When I turned toward him, his expression morphed from a stern frown to a smile.

"Sorry, Regina. I didn't recognize you."

That's right, these people know me already. "That's OK," I said, trying to look like I was on familiar ground.

"I'm Andy. The lowly second AD." Andy must have read the uncertainty in my eyes.

"I know who you are, Andy."

"Don't worry about it. You only meet, what, about a jillion people a week? Right this way, Regina. We have a chair for you."

Following Andy to a director's chair that was set up near the camera, I got a real jolt when I saw the scene that was being rehearsed. Bradley was on a blanket with Melissa, the actress who played Stephanie. The two passionately embraced as about twenty crew people watched them.

What an interesting way to make a living. That was the

first thought I had. The second was, *Melissa is one gorgeous gal*. And she certainly filled out a bikini better than I did, even in my dreams.

"All right, silence! Places, background! This is a take!" A man standing next to the camera said this. He looked really serious. Which struck me as kind of funny, because what they were about to film looked like a modern version of *Clambake*, an old Elvis Presley movie I'd seen when I was a kid.

But everyone listened to him, running this way and that, like troops getting ready for battle. A woman scooted up to Bradley and Melissa and sprayed them with a water bottle.

A guy wearing a *Spring Break Shark Attack* T-shirt walked to a spot just in front of Bradley. "Scene seventeen, take one," he said, then snapped a black-and-white clapboard with a loud *crack*.

It took them ten tries to get the scene just the way the director wanted. For one thing, Melissa kept erupting into laughter for some reason, which didn't seem to faze Bradley but really annoyed the director. So this meant there were ten more sprays from the water bottle. Ten more cracks of the clapboard. Ten more passionate kisses for Bradley.

I went into a kind of reverie as I watched the scene. First, I'll admit that I imagined myself lying on the sand in Melissa's place. (Can you blame me?) But then I mentally wandered off and thought about the life I'd been living just a few days before. Before my wish.

Band broken up. No boyfriend. No prospects. Going through the drudgery of school in the middle of a harsh winter. Now here I was, in Malibu, a famous musician, who was visiting my famous actor boyfriend and watching guys and girls run around in bathing suits. In February!

"Dinner! One hour," the serious man yelled, blasting me out of my daydream.

People took off toward the parking lot as if they were in a race. I stayed in my director's chair and watched a young girl in clam diggers hand Melissa a bathrobe. Melissa said something to Bradley, laughed, then joined the exodus to the parking lot.

Bradley smiled when he saw me. He walked slowly in my direction, toweling off the water from his muscular chest and biceps on his way. Then he put the towel around my neck, pulled me gently toward him and leaned in for a kiss. Remembering my feigned illness the previous night, he stopped a few inches from my lips and raised his eyebrows.

"How are you feeling?" he asked.

I thought about Julian and Hayley at that moment. "A whole lot better," I assured him.

Bradley nodded, then gave me a kiss. "Hi," he said.

"Hi," I said back.

Bradley took my hand and led me across the sand toward a group of trailers parked in the corner of the lot. "How'd your recording session go?"

"Good."

"Excellent. You hungry?"

I realized I was starving. "I could eat something."

"I need to change first."

It felt wonderful, being led across the sand by a gorgeous guy in a bathing suit on a beautiful February night in Malibu,

California. And yes, this is when those seven words I told you about made their first appearance, surfacing in my brain like something floating up from watery depths.

A girl could get used to this.

9

"How does it . . . feel to be . . . one of the beautiful . . .
PEOPLE?"

Still wearing his bathing suit, Bradley sang along to a CD that was playing in his laptop in his dressing room. It was a small space, so we were pretty close to one another. I smiled as he sang, but I was perplexed. Where did he get this CD of the Caverns playing "Baby, You're a Rich Man," one of the Beatles/Bloomsbury songs we had recorded for our second album?

Bradley suddenly scooted next to me on the little booth seat. "This is such a great song, Regina."

"Thanks."

"There's something really . . . *sexy* about you sharing your new songs with me. It's cool, you know? I'm the only one who's heard the new set of Regina Bloomsbury classics!"

So that was it. I'd slipped a prerelease bootleg CD of *Something New* to Bradley. That explained where he got the song, but I couldn't quite figure out why Bradley's boyish, over-the-top excitement about the CD was making me feel . . . well, kind of uncomfortable. Before I could dwell on that, however, Bradley started to sing again.

"Baby, you're a rich man / Baby, you're a rich man / BABY, YOU'RE A RICH MAN, TOO-OO!" I winced when he tried to hit the high notes. Truth be told, the guy couldn't sing a lick!

So I'd found Bradley's Achilles' heel. He wasn't perfect after all. That didn't matter to me, of course. It made him a little more human, actually.

"God, look at me. I forgot," Bradley said. "Dinnertime!"

I nodded gratefully, then waited as Bradley went into his tiny bathroom to change. He emerged wearing a pair of jeans and a plain white T-shirt. It was ridiculous how good he made a pair of jeans and a plain white T-shirt look.

"Shall we dine?" he asked cheerfully.

I didn't reply. That's because I had entered a Bradley zone. This trance was different from the one I had experienced on the beach as they shot Bradley's scene. This time I was focused on one thing, and one thing only. The teen god whose picture was plastered on girls' walls all over the world. Would I ever get used to the fact that I was actually dating this guy?

"Regina?"

Bradley Sawyer saying my name was a nice way to come back to earth. 'Cause he was actually there, in the flesh, standing only a few yards away. I took a moment to compose myself, then got up from my seat and said, "Yes, we shall."

For dinner, there was steak and salmon and rice and freshly cooked vegetables and a huge salad and, to top it off, cake and cherry pie for dessert. I was expecting, I don't know, picnic kind of food. Burgers and hot dogs and stuff like that.

"Do you always eat like this on the set?" I asked in amazement when I saw the menu written on a chalkboard at the food trailer, then quickly zipped it when I saw Bradley frown.

You've been on the P.C.H. *set before! How many times do you have to be reminded of that?*

In an attempt to change the subject, I pointed to the pier and asked, "Can we eat out there?" I could tell Bradley was still thinking about my you-always-eat-like-this? comment, but then he smiled and said, "Sure."

We found a spot and sat on the edge of the planks, our legs dangling over the water. The twinkling lights along the railing and their reflection dancing in the water below made me think Magic Time. That's what it felt like, being out on that pier with Bradley. Like a perfect moment.

"Yessiree. This is a long way from Montana," Bradley said suddenly.

I almost replied, "That's where you're from?" before catching myself. I'm telling you, it was hard to remember that I had a history with these people. I had to tread carefully in my conversations with Bradley, not knowing what he and I had already talked about.

"I still can't believe it, sometimes," Bradley continued. "I mean, can you, Regina? Can you believe what's happened to us?"

"No," I said, quite truthfully.

"It's like, the first sixteen, seventeen years of our lives, nothing happened. Then, BLAM!" Bradley laughed and shook his head at the wonder of it all.

"Well, *something* happened," I said, bristling a bit at Bradley's depiction of our lives before fame and fortune as nothing. "I mean . . . school. Parties. Girlfriends. Boyfriends."

"Yeah. All that," Bradley said dismissively.

"Can you ever imagine going back?" I asked. I surprised myself, asking that question.

"What, you mean to visit?"

"No, I guess I mean . . . do you ever think about what your life would have been like if you hadn't become famous?"

"All the time. It's my motivation. To keep going. 'Cause I never want to go back to being just a Montana boy. Besides, if I'd never come out here, we wouldn't have met."

I felt a kiss vibe coming from Bradley. He was looking at me, deep into my eyes, then he leaned in and kissed me lightly on the lips. I hesitated, then kissed him back. That led to a longer kiss.

Wow.

That describes the kiss as well as any other word I can think of. As in . . .

Wonderful.
Out of this world.
Want more of this!

I'll admit I haven't kissed that many boys—I really need to like a boy to want to kiss him—but it was pretty clear that Bradley had kissed a lot of girls. The kiss had that kind of experience behind it. But you know what? I didn't care how many girls Bradley had kissed before me. All I knew was that he was with me at this perfect moment on this perfect night, and nothing else mattered.

As the kiss was reaching its peak—that's what it felt like it was doing, anyway—it dawned on me that I was still holding my plastic fork and knife (duh!) so I tossed them aside in order to be able to put my arms around Bradley. When I reached around his neck . . .

My tray of food slipped off my lap and fell into the water! The splash was like a slap in the face. To say the moment was broken would be an understatement. We sat, silent, for a moment, then laughed. I mean, what else could we do?

"We're back!" a voice I recognized as the serious guy yelled from the beach.

"I'll say," I agreed, then we both laughed again.

"Sorry to kiss and run, Regina, but I have to get to makeup."

I nodded. "I think I'll just stay here for a bit."

Bradley smiled, gave me a quick kiss, then headed off down the pier. As I watched him go, I noticed that some of Bradley's tan had rubbed off on my jacket. He wasn't bronzed after all.

It was just make-believe.

10

Dad was waiting for me in my room when I got back from the beach. I literally jumped when I came through the door and saw him.

"What are you doing here, Dad?"

"Waiting for you." I could tell he was angry. "Where have you been?"

"I went to see Bradley on the set."

"Just like that? Without telling anyone?"

"What's the big deal?"

"For one thing, you're only sixteen. I don't care if you've been all around the world. I still want to know where you are when I'm not with you. For another, we were supposed to film the video tonight." That caught me off guard. Had that been on the itinerary? Maybe I purposely forgot to remember that it had. "You inconvenienced a lot of people tonight, Regina."

"I'm sorry, OK?" And I was. "Things have been pretty crazy this week. I guess I just blanked on the video."

"You know what? I've been holding this in, but I can't anymore. I don't like Bradley. I don't trust him. I think he's after you for all the wrong reasons."

"Why, because he didn't know me before I was famous?"

"Something like that."

"So, what are you saying? Break up with him just because you don't trust him?"

"You know I wouldn't ask you to do that. But I do wish you and Julian had stayed together."

I didn't know what to say to that, so I kept quiet. Dad sighed suddenly and ran his hand through his thinning hair. He looked older to me in that moment. I didn't like that. He stared out the window, but I got the impression he wasn't really looking at anything outside.

"You'll feel better when we get back home," I said.

"I'm not sure if *we* are going back home. That's part of the problem."

I'd forgotten about that. "You don't have to worry about that, Dad. I'm definitely going home with you on Sunday."

Dad looked at me to see if I was telling the truth. Something in my eyes must have told him that I was, because he visibly relaxed. But then he frowned and shook his head. "I don't know. I still have a bad feeling about all this. It's like the wheels are about to come off on this whole crazy ride."

"Everything's gonna be fine." I didn't say that with as much conviction. Maybe because I wasn't so sure about that myself.

"You need to tell Lorna that. She was ready to go home this morning, Regina. You have to make some kind of peace with that girl."

"I will." I said that, but making peace with Lorna was low on my list of things to do. She'd *left* the Caverns just a few days before, after all. OK, that was before my wish, but still . . .

Dad stared at me, then pushed himself up from his chair. I felt bad for him. He looked weary, and I knew it wasn't from jet lag. All this "fame" stuff had obviously taken a toll on him. As he was leaving, he said, "The video shoot is first thing tomorrow. We leave at nine."

I sat on the sofa like a lump after Dad was gone, staring out the window. I'm not the kind of person who believes in "signs," but it was kind of interesting that all I could see of the *Meet the Caverns!* billboard from where I sat was *me*. My bandmates were cropped from sight. So, there was my huge face, in half shadow, staring back at me.

It felt appropriate, that isolated image of myself. 'Cause that's how I felt. In just one day, I'd managed to get Dad, Julian, Lorna, and Danny mad at me. The only person whose feathers I hadn't ruffled was Bradley.

I smiled at the thought of Bradley. Paradise Cove had been a total blast. *So why are you getting on a plane on Sunday and leaving all of this wonderful stuff behind, Regina?*

Like a number of other questions, I stored that one in the Later Department of my brain.

The dreams started that night.

They were different from my normal dreams. It was like the difference between watching a 3-D IMAX movie and the same movie on TV. They were so "in my face," so real.

My first dream, on my second night in L.A., was a kissing one.

Bradley's lips on mine.

No, wait. Julian's.

No. Bradley's.

Julian's.

Bradley's.

It was *both* Bradley and Julian.

Morphing from one to the other.

Very strange. But not unpleasant.

Unsettling, maybe.

But definitely not unpleasant.

I was waiting in line at the Starbucks just down from our hotel the next morning when I saw Julian at a corner table by the window. His hair was all messed up and he looked like he'd just gotten up. Some guys look pretty good that way. Julian is one of them.

My first thought when I saw him was, *Should I go talk to him?* My second was . . . *of course!* I was working with Julian the rest of the week, after all. I couldn't avoid the boy. I didn't want to avoid Julian, anyway. I still needed a confidant. And I still wanted a friend.

So, when I got my coffee, I went over to Julian's table— totally aware of all the stares and whispers of "That's Regina Bloomsbury!" from people in line and at the tables—and sat down across from him. He didn't see me coming. He had been totally zeroed in on a pad of paper. There were lines scrawled in it. Lyrics, from what I could tell.

"Don't worry," I said when he looked up, surprised, from his pad. "I won't bother you. There's just . . . nowhere else to sit."

Julian studied me for a moment, then went back to his pad. OK, that was rude, but I let it pass. I sipped my coffee and watched Julian work. I had a hunch he was working on lyrics for the song I had heard him play in his room. I hummed the chorus. That got his attention.

"You remembered," he said, surprised.

"It's a catchy chorus, Julian. It's a good song." That broke the ice a bit. Julian looked genuinely pleased at my compliment. "Working on the lyrics?" Julian nodded. "I'd still like to help."

Julian's better mood changed faster than a sneeze. "Why are you doing this, Regina?"

"What?" I really didn't know what he was talking about.

"Don't be coy, OK? You don't need my song."

"It's not about needing your song, Julian. It's about wanting to work with you."

"I don't get it. Why do you want to work with me again all of a sudden?"

"I just thought . . ." I trailed off. My conversation with Julian was starting to bring me down.

"Look, why don't we just"—Julian searched for what we should just do—"be professionals this week. We'll do what we have to do. Then you can go your way, and we'll go ours."

"Oh, great! Why don't you just kick me out the door!" I could feel my cheeks burn all of a sudden, like someone had put two little hot plates on them.

"C'mon, Regina. Stop playing dumb, will you? That's what this has been leading up to and you know it!" I just sat and glared at Julian. "Oh, that's right. You have amnesia."

The way Julian said "amnesia," it was as if he were making fun of me. Like he didn't believe me. This was not the Julian

I knew and loved. The Twin Oaks Julian. It was like his evil twin or something.

"So, have fun with *Hayley* last night?" I couldn't believe it when I said that. It was so juvenile. But it was the best I could do under the circumstances.

"At least I didn't forget about the video shoot. Bradley really has his hooks in you, doesn't he?"

That did it! That's when I snapped.

"No, Julian. Bradley doesn't have his hooks in me. But I'll tell you one thing. He's the only one being nice to me lately!" I got up from the table, spilling some of my coffee in the process. "So you don't have to worry about a thing. I won't offer to help with your precious lyrics again."

I threw the rest of my coffee in the trash can on my way out of Starbucks. I didn't need it anymore. My confrontation with Julian was like a triple shot of pure caffeine. As far as I was concerned, from that moment on, it was full-speed-ahead time! Time to live my wish come true to its fullest and not care what anyone thought about me. The first stop on my new-attitude tour of L.A.?

The video shoot.

11

To be honest, the director of the video didn't have a chance.

Todd was young, twentysomething, and stood in the center of Soundstage 22 at Paramount Studios, explaining the concept of the video to me and the rest of the band. I stood to one side, apart from my bandmates, listening. No one had said a word in the limo on the way to Paramount, which was fine by me.

"So you guys are gonna be playing onstage," Todd said. "*He* will be in the crowd." The "he" referred to the title character of "He Loves You," my slightly revised version of "She Loves You," one of the Beatles' most effervescent hits and—as I had discovered on the Caverns Web site—the next single being released from *Meet the Caverns!* "As you're singing, I'll cut in scenes of you, Regina, and *He*. Flashbacks. How you two met. Your first kiss. Your first fight. We'll film those scenes later."

The soundstage had been transformed into a high school auditorium. Basketball court. Bleacher seats. A stage for the band under one of the basketball nets. Background extras stood nearby, waiting for instruction.

"What's going on over there?" I asked, referring to a chore-ographer rehearsing dancers in a corner of the soundstage. Our recording of "He Loves You" played on an amplified iPod set up near the dancers.

"They'll be doing a dance routine as you sing. OK. Any questions?" I was working up to one. Actually, it was more of a statement than a question. "Great," Todd said. "We'll get going as soon as you're through with hair and makeup."

"I'm not doing this," I declared suddenly. Todd looked at me as though I were speaking in a foreign tongue. "It's a lame concept. It's juvenile." There was a collective exhale from the band. *Here we go again* is what that sound clearly said.

Trey, who was on the periphery of our little group, listening to this, stepped between me and Todd. I think he feared a fistfight might break out between us.

"MTV wants to premiere 'He Loves You' this weekend, the day after the Grammys, Regina," Trey explained calmly. "I don't think we have time to change the concept."

"We barely have enough time as it is!" Todd jabbed, looking over Trey's shoulder. "Considering we were supposed to film this *last night!*"

"I would have felt the same way last night," I countered. "I'm not doing the video this way. It's not right for the song."

Todd glared at me, then transferred his gaze to Trey. "You're the main man, Trey. Tell us what to do."

"I'll tell you what to do," I interrupted. "Everyone take a break while I write a new concept." I spun around and headed for my dressing room, which was a trailer parked outside the soundstage.

When I got there . . . panic! I grabbed a drink from the tiny refrigerator with a trembling hand and gulped it down as I paced back and forth in the small space. Like a ghost from my not-too-distant past, my Insecure Self paced right along next to my new Confident Self.

I.S.: *What were you thinking?*

C.S.: *I couldn't help it! It was a lame concept. It would have been like a Britney Spears video!*

I.S.: *So you think you can come up with something better?*

C.S.: *I have to. I mean, how hard can it be?*

I.S.: *I don't know, but you better get cracking. There's only about a hundred people in there waiting for you!*

What were my two selves to do? Thankfully—but predictably, I suppose—the Fab Four came to our rescue. Specifically, a scene in *A Hard Day's Night* came to our rescue. For those of you who have never seen the movie, a quick explanation:

At the beginning of the movie, the Beatles travel from their hometown of Liverpool to London to make an appearance on a TV variety show. Feeling restless and cooped up in the TV studio as they wait to rehearse for that evening's performance, they charge outside and go a bit crazy in a nearby field as "Can't Buy Me Love" plays joyously on the sound track. (A scene that's credited as one of the first-ever music videos!)

Quick cuts.

Handheld shots.

Helicopter shots.

Black-and-white footage.

Perfect!

Seeing as no one had ever seen *A Hard Day's Night* before, this would be a new idea! Fueled by a fresh burst of adrenaline, I slapped a couple pieces of paper down on the little dressing room table and grabbed a pen.

OK, how to begin? (*thinking . . . thinking . . .*) Got it! Before the song kicks in, the Caverns are being told what the video is going to be by a pompous young director.

Good. Keep going.

OK, OK . . . what next? How about, the band restlessly waits to film the video as dancers rehearse their unoriginal, seen-it-all-before routine in the background.

Brilliant!

Now what? That was the easy part, thanks to *AHDN*. The Caverns can't take the boredom anymore, so they (I, we) charge from the soundstage and proceed to run amok around Paramount Studios.

I like it!

As soon as I was done writing the script, including the dialogue, I delivered it to the two Ts. Trey and Todd. One of the Ts didn't like it very much. Matter of fact, when Todd read what I wrote, he yelled, "I quit!" and stormed off the soundstage!

Silence . . .

This was my moment. I could feel it. Time for me to step up to the plate. I took a deep breath, shoved aside my Insecure Self, and offered to take over as director. I was clearly the gal for the job, I told Trey. I had the entire video in my head. Trey thought about that for a moment, then said, "Let's do it!"

It's one thing to say you're going to direct a music video. It's an altogether different thing to actually do it. I froze after hearing Trey say, "Let's do it!" A hundred pairs of eyes had instantly locked in on *moi*, all seemingly asking the same thing:

Do what?

Good question.

Say something, Regina. Anything!

"You!" I pointed to a background extra. He looked around to make sure I was talking to him. "Yeah, you. You're going to play the part of the director." The guy's face lit up like one of the old-fashioned pinball machines they have at the Twin Oaks bowling alley. "Somebody get him a script," I yelled, trying to imitate the serious guy on the set at the beach the night before.

After that outburst, I slipped on my director's hat with surprising ease. I couldn't believe how well I handled things. When people asked me questions—and they did, constantly, whether it was the cameraman, the first AD, or the costumer—I answered them right away. I guess because I knew exactly what I wanted.

It was exciting to be in the center of all of the swirling activity, let me tell you. The energy and vibes were . . . *palpable*, I believe is the word.

At one point during the shoot, guess which seven words made their second appearance. You got it.

A girl could get used to this!

And why not? I felt totally in control when I was directing the video. A new feeling for me. One that I liked. It was nice to feel so confident for a change.

So, after many handheld shots . . .

A couple of helicopter shots (Can you believe it? I asked for a helicopter and got it!) . . .

Much spontaneity and improvised goofiness from me (and halfhearted spontaneity and goofiness from my bandmates) . . .

We had the video for "He Loves You" in the can.

I found myself wondering after we had wrapped if I would still be in my wish world when "He Loves You" had its world premiere the day after the Grammys on MTV. It would be nice to see it. Especially the beginning of the video, when they show the name of the band, the song, and the director. Which would read:

"Directed by Regina Bloomsbury."

12

"I'm assuming you've made your decision?"

Trey and I were in my trailer after the filming was completed. Lorna and Danny had taken off with two of the dancers. Julian had taken off with Hayley.

Hayley. All I'll say about her is . . . what a knockout. When I saw her, my first thought was, she'd make a perfect Barbie to my Bradley's Ken. My second thought was, if Bradley and Hayley (see, even their names kind of fit together) were a couple, that would leave Julian and me . . . well, never mind. This is not the time to go there.

"Decision?" I said. I felt hyper and excited and was still on the adrenaline high my director's hat had given me.

"Yeah. *Decision*," Trey said, obviously annoyed with me. "As in, have you made the decision to move to L.A.?"

Moving? To L.A.? "I'm . . . not sure."

"Regina, listen to me." Trey waited until he had my full attention. "Please, do not get on that plane on Sunday. You hear me? If you go back to Twin Oaks, you're just postponing the inevitable. This is the perfect time to make a clean break.

I talked to your mom, and she's ready to move up here as soon as you say *L.A.*"

"She is?" I had filed Mom under Later. Hearing her name snapped me out of my jumpy, unfocused state.

"I know this is difficult. I know feelings will get hurt. But it happens all the time. Beyoncé? Justin? They both started out with groups before going solo, right? And why did they go solo? Because they're stars. So are you. Better to strike out on your own now. And I guarantee . . . after you do? You'll feel better. Who needs all this crap with Lorna, for example? I don't, that's for sure."

Trey grabbed a chair and placed it next to me. He reminded me of an eagle zeroing in on its prey. "Besides all that, you can't tell me you don't feel restricted by your dad. I mean, he still has you living in that two-bedroom house in Twin Oaks! What's that all about? You can have any place you want in L.A. You can have servants. *Anything!* Why would you want to go back to Twin Oaks? What does it have to offer you any-more?"

Actually, good question. As I thought about that . . .

"Your mom, on the other hand. What a hoot!"

I frowned. Trey said that he had talked to Mom—I was assuming on the phone, seeing as she lived in San Diego—but how well did they actually know each other?

"Your mom will definitely let you spread your wings and fly, girl." It was a jolt, hearing Trey say that. 'Cause, as I mentioned, I did feel like my dad had been trying to keep my wings clipped. "You better believe she'll let you be the sixteen-going-on-thirty-year-old woman you really are!" Trey leaned back in his chair with a smile. That turned out to be his punch line. Which was pretty lame, considering that I was hardly sixteen going on thirty. Sometimes I felt like I was sixteen going on ten.

"You only have three days until your plane takes off, Regina." The stark overhead light in the trailer caused Trey's black eyebrows to cast strange-looking, birdlike shadows downward onto his temples. "Three days and counting."

When I got back to the hotel, I took that hot tub soak I had put off the previous day. I needed to relax and think about things. The tub seemed as good a place as any to do just that.

Three days and counting.

Looking back on it, my tub soak was the tipping point in my L.A. journey. That's when I cautiously turned the wheel from "I'm just out to have a good time in L.A." and began steering toward "Wait a second here. I've been given a chance for a new life. A completely different *kind* of life. Why should I throw away such an incredible opportunity? What *does* my old Twin Oaks life have to offer me anymore?"

Misery was all I could think of.

Brinnnnng!

I picked up the phone that hung between the tub and the toilet. It was Bradley. He'd been released early from filming and had the rest of the day free.

"I want to take you somewhere," he said.

Glad to hear his voice, I asked, "And where would that somewhere be?"

"It's a surprise. Not the special one I promised. This is just a little surprise."

"I love surprises," I said, thinking how good and comfortable it felt talking to this guy.

"Good. Can you be ready in a few?"

"I can," I said.

And I was.

13

"Look! There's Fay Wray!"

I dashed gleefully to the grave site and stood in front of it. Bradley's surprise turned out to be a visit to the Hollywood Forever Cemetery. "You've never been? It's a *must*," he had told me after revealing our destination. We had walked around for about a half hour and visited the grave sites of Mel Blanc (the voice of Bugs Bunny and Daffy Duck), Bugsy Siegel (a notorious real-life gangster who was played by Warren Beatty in a movie), Peter Lorre (one of the greatest of all Hollywood character actors), and now Fay Wray, King Kong's one true love.

The cemetery was very old-school. The reason I knew so many of the actors buried there was because my dad is a movie junkie and had brought me up on a steady diet of some of the greatest Hollywood flicks ever made. As I looked down at Ms. Wray's name on the simple marker set among the neatly trimmed grass, Bradley came up behind me and put his arms around my waist.

I smiled and leaned my head back against Bradley's

shoulder. I was enjoying being with him. Something had begun to stir in me, that's for sure. Something different and new . . . that tipping point I mentioned. It was like I had begun to break out of my Twin Oaks shell and was looking around at L.A.—this *new world*—less as a place to visit and more like . . . the future, maybe?

Looking around the cemetery, I saw groups of people checking out their brochures to see where their favorite movie stars were buried. "Something tells me a cemetery isn't exactly an appropriate place for public displays of affection, Bradley."

"You're absolutely right." Bradley immediately released me and moved away. When I turned and looked at him, he was smiling.

"What's with that smile, Mr. Sawyer?"

"Oh, nothing."

"Yeah, right."

Something was suddenly bouncing back and forth between us, and it was pretty electric. Bradley fixed his gaze on me and I felt myself swooning. I really did. There was a reason Bradley had been referred to as the next Brad Pitt. He had that kind of raw star power, and he knew it. I felt a sudden urge to run and jump into his arms, but held back. Good thing, too, because just then Bradley gave me a nod, indicating that I should take a look behind me.

When I did, I saw a family of four approaching us with shy and excited smiles. Actually, the dad didn't look all that excited, but his wife and two kids—the kids looked to be in their early teens—certainly were.

"Could we possibly get a picture of you two together?" the mother asked hopefully.

"Of course," Bradley said, instantly camera-ready. He put his arm around me and smiled his gorgeous smile. I managed what felt like an awkward sort of smile as the wife and her daughter took their pictures.

"Now how about one with Regina and me and your two great-looking kids?" Bradley suggested. The daughter was beside herself with glee. Her brother tried to act cool, but I could tell he was pretty excited, too. After the mother took a couple of pictures, Bradley said, "OK, that'll be fifty dollars."

The mother's mouth literally fell open in shock. "Just kidding!" Bradley said. The mother responded with an embarrassed little you-got-me-there! laugh, then said, "Thanks so much."

"Our pleasure," Bradley said. He was really good at this part of being famous, that's for sure.

"I watch your show every Thursday!" the girl said as the foursome walked away.

"Excellent!" Bradley replied.

The boy didn't say anything, but he was still staring at me as he and his family disappeared around the nearby mausoleum.

Bradley took my hand then and led me away from Fay Wray's grave. "Gotta be nice to the fans. Even when you don't feel like it. One of the golden rules of being a celebrity."

"Looked to me like you felt like it," I said, giving him a playful nudge with my hip.

"*Please.* That's the last thing I felt like doing back there."

"Really?" I said, genuinely surprised. "You're a pretty good actor, then."

Like he had done in my hotel room that first night, Bradley held out his hands in a way that said, *Hey, I'm Bradley Sawyer!*

Bradley owned a beautiful black '65 Corvette Sting Ray convertible, which he confided had cost him an obscene amount of money. As he drove the car up into the Hollywood Hills—with the top down—I lounged in the passenger seat, squinting happily up into the sun. What an absolutely incredible place L.A. was turning out to be. It made living where the temperature could sometimes plunge to minus ten degrees seem downright barbaric, that's for sure.

When it looked like the narrow, winding street Bradley was navigating couldn't go any higher, he turned into a driveway. We had arrived at his house. Appropriately, you could see the famous **HOLLYWOOD** sign from Bradley's front yard. Well, not the entire sign. Just the **HOLLY** part.

Reminding myself that I had probably been to Bradley's house before, I held back from saying what a great place he had when we went inside. But it was a great place. It looked like something you'd see in *House Beautiful*. If Bradley had paid an obscene amount of money for his Corvette, his house and the stuff in it must have cost, I don't know, quadruple that.

"Want anything to drink?" Bradley asked as he went into the kitchen.

"Pop, if you have some," I called out to him.

Bradley laughed.

"They call that soda out here, Regina. But, yes, I do have pop. I have everything here."

We'd been yelling back and forth, so I went into the kitchen, leaned up against the counter, and watched Bradley get the drinks out of his black refrigerator. Just to his right, a wall of windows framed the backyard, which was really beautiful. Flowers everywhere. A black-bottomed Jacuzzi. A couple of cool-looking sculptures.

Bradley kicked the refrigerator door shut with his foot, took a sip of whatever he was drinking as he walked around the counter, and handed me a glass of, OK, soda. Before I was able to take a drink, Bradley had placed his glass on the counter and had his arms around my waist.

"What do you think you're doing, mister?"

"If I'm not mistaken, we were interrupted in the middle of something last night on the pier. Not to mention at the cemetery today."

"If you had tried to kiss me in the cemetery, I would have definitely stopped you."

"Right, seeing as a cemetery isn't the proper place for public displays of affection." Bradley smiled and pulled me closer to him. "But my house is."

"But then it's not a public display, is it?"

"Aaahhh . . ."

I put down my drink, raised up on tiptoe, and kissed Bradley. I kissed first, this time, and I think it caught Bradley off guard. But he recovered pretty fast and started driving the bus, so to speak, and I was totally in a Bradley zone when his cell phone started to play "He Loves You."

I was sure Bradley would just ignore it, but he instantly pulled away and retrieved the phone from his pocket. "Nice ring tone, huh?" he said with a smile. Checking out the name on the display, Bradley announced that it was Melissa. "Hey, girlfriend! What's up?"

Girlfriend? I thought with a frown. *What's with that? He was just in the middle of kissing me, and now he's calling Melissa "girlfriend"?*

Bradley listened for a moment, then said, "Sure, c'mon over. Regina's here." Bradley laughed at something Melissa said, at the same time rolling his eyes for my benefit. "Of course. The more the merrier. See you soon." Bradley snapped his cell shut. "Melissa's bringing some friends over. Cool with you?"

"Melissa? That would be your girlfriend?"

"What's wrong with you? You know that's her nickname ever since we became girlfriend/boyfriend on the show."

Oh . . . OK.

Bradley tapped the iPhone screen a couple of times. "I'm gonna call my posse. I'm smelling a party here!"

Bradley looked pretty pumped about that. I definitely wasn't. After leaving the cemetery, Bradley had asked if I wanted to go to his house, hang out, maybe watch a movie on his huge flat-screen TV with the "killer" sound system. Considering how crazed things had been from the moment I touched down in L.A., a little alone time with Bradley sounded absolutely great.

So I was pretty disappointed when Bradley seemed to just forget about the idea of us hanging out and maybe watching a movie later on. After all, we'd been having such a great time with just the two of us.

But here's the thing. I'd only spent a little time with Bradley, but already I could see that he and I were different in more ways than one. For one thing, Bradley gave off a party maestro kind of vibe. He moved with that kind of energy. As for me? Not a party girl. The few I'd been to in Twin Oaks seemed, I don't know, just frantic or something. So a bunch of people coming over to Bradley's? Not my idea of a good time.

But as Bradley talked and laughed on his phone, I gave myself a sudden mental slap. *Stop it, girl! This is your wish-come-true Grammy week. Have some fun for gosh sakes. And don't be afraid to try some new things!*

Yeah, like party with rich, famous, and beautiful teen-agers. Who wouldn't want to do that? I thought I could maybe get into that, if I tried.

Bradley had finished up with one member of his posse and was calling another when my cell phone rang. My "hello" was immediately followed by "Where are you, Regina?!"

My heart did a backflip at the sound of my dad's angry voice. What had I forgotten this time?

"If you're not in Burbank in half an hour, the Caverns go on without you! Understand?!"

Oh, no. The *Tonight Show*! *That's* what I'd forgotten! "I'll be right there!" I shouted into the cell, then quickly pocketed it before Dad had a chance to yell at me some more. I franti-cally waved my hands in front of Bradley's face to interrupt his phone call.

"Just a sec," Bradley told his friend, then he gave me a frown. "What's up?"

"I forgot about the *Tonight Show*!"

"What?"

"The Caverns are on the *Tonight Show* tonight. It starts in half an hour!"

"You forgot about the *Tonight Show*?"

"That's what I just said!"

"How could you forget about the *Tonight Show*, Regina? That's, like, really huge!"

"I know! I know!"

"Party's off, dude!" Bradley yelled into his cell. "Give Melissa a call, will you? I have to get Regina to the *Tonight Show*!"

We charged out of the house, and I jumped into Bradley's Corvette. Instead of getting into the car, Bradley pressed the garage door opener that was attached to the driver's-side sun visor. "This won't get us there fast enough," Bradley said.

As the garage door opened, I had the irrational thought that Bradley had a small airplane stashed away and that he was going to fly me to Burbank. There was no airplane, of course, but there was a sleek-looking motorcycle.

"Ready to make some time?" Bradley asked with a rakish grin.

Before I knew it, we were blasting down the Hollywood Hills and leaning crazily from one side to the other, as Bradley took the curves at breathtaking speed. At one point, I laughed out loud it was so exciting. And then I thought, *This ride perfectly captures how I'm feeling right now. Breathless and traveling too fast and throwing caution to the wind!*

Because at that point, I have to admit I was totally falling for Bradley Sawyer, even though I knew I shouldn't be. It was obvious that Bradley shared at least a few characteristics with

Zane, his alter ego on *P.C.H.* He struck me as that kind of smooth operator and was maybe dating me for all the wrong reasons—just like my dad said.

But let me tell you, when you fall into the orbit of someone as powerfully magnetic as Bradley Sawyer, it's hard to resist the pull of gravity. I certainly couldn't. But as we flew down the twisting street and I was holding on to Bradley for dear life and the wind rushed past, making it feel like we were in the middle of a really intense storm, I gave myself this warning:

Be careful, Regina. You're a small-town girl, remember. Pull out now or put on your life vest. 'Cause you're definitely getting in over your head on this one!

14

"Ladies and gentlemen! Please welcome the multiplatinum-selling, nominated-for-seven-Grammy-Awards, straight-outta-Twin-Oaks sensation . . . the Caverns!"

The small audience stood and yelled. I counted out the beat for "He Loves You," and we jumped into the song with all the verve we could manage at five thirty in the afternoon.

I hadn't had time to change or go to makeup after Bradley dropped me off at NBC. My stern-faced dad, who was waiting for me outside the building (one look at him, and Bradley said, "Call you later!"), quickly led me past a couple of security guards, down a labyrinth of halls, through several doors, and to the backstage area of the *Tonight Show*.

Julian, Lorna, and Danny were already positioned on the stage, ready to play. As I strapped on my guitar and rushed to the center microphone, I thought, *Everything looks so small!* The stage. The studio. The audience. Compared to what it looked like on TV . . . this was Tiny Town. Then, before I had time to even get nervous, Chris Rock made his intro, and we were off and running.

In spite of how rushed and crazed I was, I played the heck out of that song, if I do say so myself. Maybe the fact that I *was* so rushed and crazed is the reason I played with such enthusiasm, the adrenaline already pumping through my body—thanks to my thrilling motorcycle ride with Bradley—before I had even hit the stage.

The band, in spite of not feeling too good about me at that point, seemed to plug into my whirlwind energy, and we wound up rocking the song especially hard. I know that audiences on live TV shows are instructed when and where to applaud even if they don't feel like it, so I was surprised at the reaction from the audience when we hit the final chord. It was really raucous and seemed totally genuine.

As soon as we were done with the song, Chris came over to the band and shook my hand as he announced, "We'll be right back!" Then he leaned in close to my ear so I could hear over all the cheering and clapping and said, "Sit closest to the desk for the interview part, okay?"

I nodded, then Chris indicated to the rest of the band to follow him. I sat on the stuffed chair next to the desk and avoided looking at the rest of the band as they squeezed onto the sofa. Before he began the interview for the audience, Chris gave us one of his infectious smiles and said, "That was cool, guys." We all smiled in return and nodded and said thanks, then a guy behind a video camera gave Chris the signal that we were back on the air.

(All this went by in a blur, believe me.)

"So, Regina, why were you so late getting here?"

That's the question Chris asked me as soon as we were

back, and it definitely threw me. But it wasn't like Chris was upset or anything. When the audience laughed, he explained, "She was. She got here just before they had to go on. Has your life become that busy?"

"It's a long way from Twin Oaks, that's for sure," I said.

"How long?" Chris asked. "I mean, what's the biggest way your life has changed since you've become so famous?"

I thought before answering. How *had* things changed for me over the past three days? "Everything seems more complicated." Which was true.

"Complicated?"

"Yeah. The life of a teenager in Twin Oaks is pretty straight-forward, you know?"

"I can imagine. So how did you turn that straightforward life into so many great songs?"

"I wasn't that in demand before all of this. So, I had plenty of time to write them."

Laughter! I smiled and looked out at the audience. It felt good, and unexpected, that laughter. It made me feel comfortable and relaxed and wanting *more* laughs.

"You're only sixteen, Regina. 'Yesterday.' 'In My Life.' A lot of people have commented on how mature those songs are. Especially considering how young you are."

"Yeah, it's a nice compliment. I think." I scrunched up my face in an exaggerated frown, signalling that I really wasn't sure whether or not it was a compliment. More laughter from the audience, which was good because it seemed to distract Chris from asking any more questions about how I came up with my supposedly original songs.

"How many here watched the Caverns' concert on MTV this past weekend?" Chris asked the audience. After the crowd had applauded their response, Chris said, "I liked the two new songs you played from your next CD. It doesn't sound to me like you're slippin' none. You have a name for the new CD?"

"*Something New.*"

"Well, I'm sure you're gonna be asked back to the show next year when *Something New* is up for *ten* Grammys. Think you can make it on time, Regina?"

I smiled and said, "Yes. Next time, I'll get here early. I promise."

"Ladies and gentlemen, Regina Bloomsbury and the Caverns!"

The audience clapped, and I waved as Chris announced who was going to be on the show the following night and the house band kicked in, and before I knew it, the show was over, and the audience was being shown the door by ushers in uniforms. A few tried to get autographs, but they were blocked off by the ushers. I was disappointed that our time on the show had to end so quickly. I felt like I was just getting warmed up!

But end it did, then we all piled into the limo and headed back to the hotel. Unfortunately, that's when all the groovy vibes from the show disappeared. Just like *that*. Yes, folks, that's when Lorna and I finally had it out. After giving each other a couple of warm-up jabs the previous few days . . .

It was all-out catfight time!

15

The silence had hung heavy in the limo for a few minutes before Lorna got things going. Nobody said, "Good gig" or "We really rocked it" or "Good vocals, Gina." There was just this awkward nothing going on. It felt like the space between me and my dad and the rest of the band was real and solid somehow and would have prevented me from getting any closer to anyone, even if I had felt like it. Which I didn't.

"Well, somebody finally said out loud what everyone else has been thinking." That was Lorna's opening line. "Regina Bloomsbury and the Caverns," she continued, with that sarcastic tone in her voice. "Millions of people will hear Chris Rock say that tonight. It's like an announcement. Lorna and Julian and Danny have officially become Regina's backup band." Lorna practically spit out the last two words, like they were a disease.

"I didn't tell him to say that," I countered, feeling hot all of a sudden.

"You didn't have to. It's the way you've been acting."

"Give me a break, Lorna. How about the way you've been

acting? Huh? How about that? Throwing me glares and sarcastic remarks ever since we took off from Twin Oaks."

"OK, ladies. Calm down." That was Dad. He sounded weary and not very convincing and ready to give up on the whole Caverns thing.

"I don't feel like calming down." And I didn't. I felt like I was wound up and ready to take off like a rocket. "I'm sick of your attitude, Lorna." I could feel Julian and Danny tense in their leather seats nearby. *Oh, boy*, their body language said. *Here we go!*

"You're sick of *my* attitude?" Lorna, who was sitting across and a little ways up from me, edged closer. "You stuck-up little princess! You don't want anybody else's original songs on our albums. You tell us exactly what to play. You forget about video shoots. You're late for the *Tonight Show*, and it's like, 'Isn't that cute. You must be so busy these days, Regina.' If I did that, I'd be fired."

"Maybe you should be," I warned.

"That's enough, Regina," Dad said. He had more force behind that command.

"You're lucky I asked you to come back to the band after you and Danny quit." At least I figured that's what had happened.

Lorna seemed at a loss for words after my last insult, so instead, she threw the soda she was drinking in my face and yelled, "Bitch!"

Stunned and outraged at the spray of soda that splashed my face, I launched myself at Lorna. She fell back from the force of my attack, quickly recovered, threw me to the floor, and pounced on top of me.

Ring the bell! Round One!

"Bitch!" . . . yanks on each other's hair . . . "BITCH!" . . . slapping and kicking . . . "[Fill in your favorite insult here. We probably said it!]" . . . hands trying to separate us . . . "BEEEE-ITCHHH!!!"

Believe it or not, as I rolled around on the floor, I thought, *This feels good!* Fighting Lorna was a wonderful release from all of the tension and craziness of my L.A. journey. It didn't occur to me that rolling on the floor of a block-long white Hummer, wrestling Lorna, was the crowning achievement, the Everest of craziness of the journey so far.

To be honest, Lorna gave as good as she got. Maybe even more so. By the time Abernathy had pulled onto the side of the freeway and helped restore order by hauling Lorna and me out of the limo by the backs of our T-shirts (he was a big, powerful guy with massive hands), I could feel a trickle of warm blood running down my cheek.

Lorna and I huffed as if we'd just run a marathon and shot eye daggers at each other. The fight hadn't gone out of us, but there was no way we could resume our battle with Abernathy's huge bulk between us.

"I do not allow fighting in my limo," he announced. "Understand?"

Dad had followed Abernathy out of the limo and stood nearby, his arms crossed. Julian sat on the floor of the limo, his legs dangling through the open back door. He looked like a spectator, ready for Round Two. Danny peeked through the tinted glass from inside the Hummer, only his nose visible from where I stood.

"*Understand?*" Abernathy repeated.

I finally nodded. Abernathy stared at Lorna. After she gave a barely perceptible nod, he announced, "One of you is riding up front with me." He didn't release me from his grasp until I said, "I will," then he continued to hold on to Lorna until I had gotten into the front passenger seat.

The glass divider was up for the rest of the journey back to the Sheraton, so I couldn't hear if anything was being said about me on the way. I didn't care. After my rumble with Lorna, I felt I had crossed some kind of invisible line. This was not a tipping point anymore. I was on the other side, baby! And I knew . . . in that moment, no way was I getting on a plane on Sunday with Lorna and Dad and the rest of the band and going back to Twin Oaks.

Calm down, Regina, my rational side urged. *This is not the time to be making such decisions.*

Yes, it is! my full-speed-ahead side countered. *Why should I go home? Tell me that? Everything I need is right here in L.A. Everything. Why should I leave all this behind? So that I can go back to being a lonely, frustrated, unconfident Twin Oaks teenager?*

My rational side was silent.

When Abernathy pulled up to the Sheraton entrance, I waited until Dad and the band were in the hotel before getting out of the limo. I looked at Abernathy before heading into the hotel. He raised his eyebrows at me in a way that asked, *What on earth was that all about?*

"I guess a girl can only take so much," I said.

"You talkin' about yourself or Lorna?"

"Me."

"Get back in here. I got something for that cut."

I slid back into the limo, relieved that Abernathy was not going to lecture me. I didn't need a lecture. I needed clarity. On my third day in L.A., I felt like I had found it.

Directing the music video . . .

My talk with Trey . . .

My motorcycle ride with Bradley . . .

The *Tonight Show* . . .

My fight with Lorna . . .

All that added up to one thing:

Do not get on that plane on Sunday!

As Abernathy treated my battle wound, the paparazzi were snapping away nearby. I didn't mind that they were capturing me in such a vulnerable moment. Matter of fact, I kind of liked it. Another thing I liked? Seeing myself up on the gigantic billboard of the Caverns. It was kind of cool being larger than life, I decided. In a sudden out-of-body experience, I actually imagined myself up on the billboard, looking out across the landscape of La-la Land.

Aaahh, yes! L.A.

This was *my* town!

16

Buzzing with my new revelation—*I'm* supposed *to stay in L.A. That's what my wish come true has been about all along*—I got into the elevator and pressed 10. By the time the doors opened on my floor, I was totally spent. It was like my energy—going down?—had drained in inverse proportion to the elevator going up. Which was no surprise. After all, what a day! As I walked to my room, visions of a long restorative night's sleep began to envelope me like warm flannel bunny PJs.

"Regina!"

I turned to see a boy, fourteen or so, peeking out from behind a slightly opened door with STAIRWAY printed on it. His hair was Beatles-style (or rather, Caverns-style), and he wore a Caverns T-shirt. He offered me a small package. "I was hoping you might take a listen to my CD," the boy whispered.

I didn't feel like dealing with a possibly crazed fan, so I said, "You know what? You're not supposed to be here. This floor is off-limits." Then I continued on my way without taking the kid's CD.

"Please?" the kid said plaintively. "There're only six songs on the CD. But they're good. They're *really good!*"

That did it. Spinning around, I angrily replied, "I'm tired! Can't you see that?! You're trespassing! Send the CD to my manager!" I was about to turn away when I saw the desperate look in the kid's eyes. I sighed wearily, then retraced my steps and took the CD, which was wrapped in plain brown paper. "What's your name?" I asked.

"Stuart."

"What's your band's name?"

"I don't have a band. I wrote all of those songs myself. I play all the instruments."

"A regular Paul McCartney, huh," I said with a smile.

"Who?"

Right. I still hadn't gotten used to the fact that the Beatles were unknown in this world. "Just someone I used to know," I explained.

"My name and number are on the CD. Can you give me a call after you've listened to it? Maybe you'd like to record some of my songs!"

Before I could answer, metallic-sounding footsteps rang out from down below. Stuart's eyes bugged out. "Gotta go! Thanks, Regina! I love you! I love your music. You're awesome!" As Stuart ran up the stairs, he held his hand up to his ear like a phone and mouthed the words, "Call me!"

A security guard appeared a few seconds later, huffing it up the stairs. He stopped when he saw me, looking grateful for the break from his stairway climb. "You see a kid around here, miss?" he gasped. "Wearing a Caverns T-shirt?"

"No," I said, slowly concealing the CD.

The guard looked skeptical of my answer. But before

reluctantly continuing his chase, he said, "By the way, my daughter's a big fan."

I waved to the guard as he pulled himself up the final flight of stairs, then let the stairway door close. *Whew!* I thought as I finally approached my room at the end of the hall. *No wonder celebs get tired of fans. They're relentless.* But fans came with the fame. And if I was staying in L.A., I'd have to learn to deal with them, the way Bradley did so well.

For now, however . . . sleep. That's all I wanted at that point. I needed to recharge. After all, it was Grammy rehearsal tomorrow! But, as it turned out, my busy day wasn't over. Not just yet. Because, waiting for me in my room . . .

Was Mom.

17

"Regina!" Mom squealed from the sofa, where she was crashed out, watching TV.

Whoa! That's Mom? I froze at the sight of my long-departed mother. Then I quickly reminded myself, *This is not the first time you've seen her in more than three years.*

In my pre-wish world, it had been more than three years since Mom had returned to Twin Oaks for a visit. A visit that was so awkward and unpleasant that she'd never been back since.

That was then, however, and this was now. My smile felt plastered on as Mom came around the sofa and hugged me. The hug gave me a moment to collect myself. I was flustered and exhausted, and the main thing that kept going through my mind was, *She's had a lot of work done!*

Mom looked much younger than she did the last time I'd seen her, and that was weird. But I couldn't show my shock. So I hugged Mom back, and in spite of all the conflicting feelings battling it out inside me, a warm glow was starting to make its presence felt by the nearness of Mom.

"What happened to you?" she asked after our hug.

"What—," I replied. Mom touched the small bandage on my forehead. "Oh! I got in a fight with Lorna."

"You're kidding me." I shook my head no. "That girl's gotta go!"

"I think she may already be," I said.

"Good! Nobody messes with my daughter and gets away with it! Hey, are you hungry?"

Like my phone conversation with her a few days before, I felt like I was talking to a kid. Mom had a young way of talking. Short. Declarative. Sentences. Hopped from one topic. To the next. Without taking a breath.

"I could eat something," I said.

"Good! 'Cause I already ordered room service. I love room service! Don't you?"

It was one of those questions that didn't really require an answer. Besides, my attention had been diverted to my bed, which was littered with paper.

"What's all that?" I asked.

"Homes! I spent the afternoon touring Beverly and Hollywood hills. We can look at them while we eat."

And we did. Mom had ordered a feast, believe me. Money (my money, I figured) was clearly no object, whether it was a room service dinner or a home she had her sights set on.

She is so the opposite of Dad, I thought as we sat on my bed and ate our endless meal and worked our way through the stack of brochures she had collected that afternoon.

I have to say, it was fun being with Mom. It didn't feel like a mother and daughter reunion after a very long time. It felt more like a pajama party, the kind I used to have with my old friend Erin before our friendship sort of dissolved, for no particular reason that I can remember. And it was a kick looking at the houses. Even though it was fantasy time. I mean, check out how much they cost!

$8,999,000. $10,599,000. $12,399,000. And that was just getting warmed up!

"This is my favorite," Mom said, handing me a brochure with a picture of a two-story, Tudor-style house. "You have to see it in person to really appreciate it." The yard looked like a park, with a beautiful pool in the shape of a guitar right in the middle of it. The house didn't look even close to being a Cher-style mansion, but still it cost . . .

"Fifteen million dollars?!" I exclaimed, laughing.

"You don't even realize it, do you, Regina?"

"Realize what?"

"You can afford this!"

"No, I can't."

Mom shook her head earnestly. "You can. This is what I've been trying to tell you. What Trey has been trying to tell you. Your dad isn't being straight with you. He's not letting you know how much you've been making this past year. He thinks it's better if you live a normal life." Mom used her fingers like quotation marks when she said, "normal life." "But you left normal a long time ago. Why live like everyone else?"

Mom didn't know it, but she was reinforcing something I had already begun thinking about. And I have to say, I got a real tingle of excitement as I stared at the brochure. I could actually live in such a luxurious place? Unbelievable!

"Let's go out and celebrate!" Mom said suddenly.

"Celebrate? What?"

"Everything! Us being together again. All your Grammy nominations. You coming to live in L.A."

"How do you know whether or not I've decided to move to L.A.?" Mom smiled a reply. "What's with that smile?" I asked.

"I went to see Miss Madison," Mom explained.

"And she would be?"

"My psychic adviser. And she told me you're definitely moving here."

"*Mom!*" I scolded. "You give your hard-earned money to a shyster psychic?"

In response to my question, Mom gave me a playful push. "She's *not*"—I pushed her back—"a *shyster*"—Mom grabbed a pillow and hit me—"*psychic!*" I grabbed a pillow and hit Mom back. We both leaped to our feet and started whaling at each other.

Pillow fight!

We were laughing and smacking each other with the pillows when . . .

Knock. Knock. Knock.

Mom collapsed onto the bed as I hopped off to get the door. Wouldn't you know, it was Dad. Talk about a mood changer.

"Hello, Richard," Mom said after what felt like about forty-five minutes of silence. She hadn't moved from the bed.

"I thought you were coming up tomorrow," Dad replied curtly.

"Changed my mind."

After another forty-five minutes went by, I said, *"Any-way . . ."*

"I wanted to talk to you, Regina, about your little altercation. But I guess this isn't the time."

"Lorna should be kicked out of the band!" Mom yelled.

"Mom. Please." I felt more like the mother of the duo than the daughter.

"She doesn't have to be kicked out," Dad replied. "She quit."

"Good!" Mom exclaimed.

"Mom. Do I have to send you back to your room?"

"You've gotten so snippy since you became famous. I love it!"

"You OK?" Dad asked, looking at my bandage.

"Yeah. Abernathy fixed me up."

Dad was silent. He hadn't come in from the hallway and didn't seem inclined to at this point. "We'll talk tomorrow. I called Trey. He's going to find a temporary bass player for the Grammys."

I think Dad wanted me to say, "I'll talk to Lorna," but I wasn't about to do that. So when I just said, "OK," Dad nodded reluctantly, gave me a "Night, Regina," and walked off down the hall.

I closed the door and leaned against it, looking at Mom.

"Let's get out of here," she said as she leaped off the bed. She was quite nimble for her age.

"I'm beat, Mom. I'm going to bed."

"What?! Don't be a party pooper, Regina. Or whatever it is you kids call a party pooper these days."

"Drag-ass might be the word."

"OK. So, don't be a drag-ass, Regina."

"I'm going to bed," I repeated firmly. "I have the Grammy rehearsal tomorrow. You know how important that is? And then I'm probably going to the *P.C.H.* set after that." Bradley had asked me to come by and visit him.

"How's Bradley? I *love* that guy! I was so happy when you dumped Julian."

I practically winced when Mom said that. "Bradley's fine," I said. Then I opened the door for Mom to leave.

"Look at you. You've become so grown-up!" Mom smiled and kissed me on the cheek. "I think that's what I've been waiting for, Regina." Mom was suddenly serious. "For you to grow up, you know? I'm not all that good with kids, to be honest. But then, you know that, don't you?"

I didn't answer. We had suddenly veered into emotional territory that I wanted to get to, eventually, with Mom. But now that she had steered us to it, I didn't know if I was ready for it.

"Anyway, I can't tell you how much it means to me that we've reconnected. I'm going to do everything I can to make it up to you. To wipe out all those bad years. OK?"

Mom had tears in her eyes all of a sudden. And just like that, so did I. We hugged, then Mom brushed a tear away from her cheek and said, "Enough of this, huh? I'm more comfortable having pillow fights."

"That was fun, Mom."

"See you tomorrow."

I nodded, then watched Mom walk off in the opposite direction that Dad had gone. Being with her for just that little while seemed to have wiped out a bit of the pain I'd been carrying for so many years. I felt lighter all of a sudden.

Not too surprising, then, that when I went to bed that night, the brochure for the Tudor house with the guitar-shaped pool was propped up prominently on the nearby nightstand. Right next to the Regina Bloomsbury Beatle doll I had tossed into my suitcase just before leaving for L.A.

18

Mom was back first thing the next morning, knocking on my door and insisting that we needed to see the Beverly Hills house sooner than later because a place like that wouldn't be on the market for very long. The Grammy rehearsal wasn't until the afternoon, so I figured, why not? I wanted to spend a little more time with Mom anyway, and this seemed like a fun way to do that.

So Abernathy took the two of us to Beverly Hills, and we met the real estate agent, who showed us through the ten-bedroom, twelve-bathroom house. Seriously, that's how many bedrooms and bathrooms were in the place. Not to mention a screening room that looked like a small movie theater, plus a bowling alley! After the amazing house tour, the agent took us out into the backyard.

I could just pitch a tent and live here! I thought as I looked around at the gorgeous expanse of green with the blue guitar-shaped pool right in the middle.

"Well, what do you think?" the real estate agent asked with a confident smile.

"The place is really big," I replied.

"Regina," my mom said in a scolding tone of voice.

"What? It is."

"Excuse us for a moment," Mom told the agent, then she took me by the arm and led me toward the pool. "You need this kind of room, girl."

"I do?"

"Absolutely. You'll have to wipe out at least a couple of bedrooms so you can build your own recording studio."

"I'm going to build my own recording studio?"

"Of course! That's what Trey said you should do when I told him we were going to look at this place."

"When did you see Trey?"

"Last night. After you turned me down for a night on the town."

"Oh." I'm not sure what bothered me more. Mom and Trey hanging out together or the fact that it wasn't difficult for me to picture the two of them hanging out together. "OK, well, let's see, that would leave me with . . . another eight bedrooms."

"This house is a really good investment, besides. You need to think about that, too. That's one of the things I love about Bradley."

"Which would be?"

"He's really smart with his money. For such a young guy, especially. That house of his? The artwork? The original Stickley furniture?"

"Maybe he's just showing off."

"That's a terrible thing to say about your boyfriend!"

"Just kidding, Mom."

"Well, don't kid like that. This is serious."

The real estate agent had edged closer to us as we talked. When she caught our attention, she smiled that confident smile again.

"So, have we made a decision, Regina?" Mom asked.

I exhaled loudly and looked around the backyard. I still had a hard time believing that I could actually afford such an expensive place. Then something occurred to me. "I should probably talk to Dad first."

"We discussed that just last night," Mom said in exasperation. "You know exactly what he would say."

I was feeling a lot of pressure from Mom to make an on-the-spot decision. As for the agent, she actually didn't seem too concerned whether I took the house or not. Probably had people coming to look at it after Mom and I left. "How's this?" I suggested. "I'll make a decision right after the Grammys. They're tomorrow night, so that means less than forty-eight hours from now."

That seemed like a safe and practical thing to say, but Mom got such a disappointed look on her face that I felt sorry for her. It was weird, the way Mom was acting more like the kid. With me in the grown-up role. Well, grown-ups always want to make their kids happy, don't they? At least I thought that was the way it was supposed to be.

So I smiled and said, "You know what? I don't think I need to wait. I'll take it!"

Mom squealed in delight and threw her arms around me. The real estate agent nodded, cool as can be, and said, "Congratulations. You've made an excellent choice."

19

I was standing backstage at the Shrine Auditorium, watching Madonna as she disappeared into the crowd that surrounded us, still in disbelief about what had just happened. A few moments before, Madonna had come right up to me, introduced herself, and told me that *Meet the Caverns!* was one of the best albums she'd ever heard. I was so stunned I didn't know what to say. Madonna was totally cool, and after giving me a few pointers on how to deal with the sudden crush of fame, she urged me to keep up the good work, then headed off when someone came up to tell her she was needed onstage.

Incredible!

Actually, Madonna was just one of the music greats I'd met since arriving at the Shrine. Mom and I had returned from our house-buying expedition a bit late (I asked Mom not to say anything to Dad about it for the time being), so Abernathy had to floor it to get Dad and me and the rest of the Caverns (minus Lorna) to the Shrine on time, which I don't think he appreciated. After we were dropped off behind the auditorium, we entered through the backstage door as an army of paparazzi furiously snapped away from a nearby street.

A slightly out-of-control, partylike atmosphere permeated the backstage area. People with headsets ran around trying to inflict some kind of order. There actually wasn't much for us to do after arriving except wait, so that had given me plenty of time to rubberneck and meet famous musicians and singers.

Beyoncé. Bruce Springsteen. Norah Jones. Rivers Cuomo.

I felt like I was in one of those movie scenes where the camera moves around the actor in a circle, over and over. It was disorienting but exciting, and things didn't stop for even a second.

Trey, who had been waiting at the backstage door for us when we arrived, never left my side. He was like my own personal Grammy tour guide, introducing me to people, pointing out producers who wanted to work with me, steering me away from people he didn't want me to meet for some reason.

I don't know where Dad and Julian and Danny were during all this. We hadn't spoken on the way to the Shrine. None of them seemed to want to dip their toes into the murky waters of the Lorna situation. I certainly didn't, so I was perfectly happy to just sit with my face buried behind the trades as I rode in the limo to the Grammy rehearsal.

Anyway, it was shortly after I'd met Madonna that the Caverns got the nod to rehearse "Hello, Goodbye." I was stunned when we were led to the Shrine stage by one of the headset people. The auditorium, with its double balconies and sweeping rows of seats, was massive. And very intimidating.

I can't pull this off! It's too much! Too overwhelming! That's what I was nervously thinking as I walked to the microphone in the middle of the stage, strapping on my guitar as I went.

Playing on the T.J. stage, in the recording studio, and on the *Tonight Show* hadn't prepared me for this. The Shrine was the BIG TIME. Literally.

I was snapped out of my jittery thoughts by some unseen person who spoke to us over a speaker. "Hello, Caverns!" the voice boomed. I waved lamely at the empty auditorium. I suddenly felt like Dorothy meeting the Wizard. "You are opening tomorrow night's Grammy Awards," the voice announced. "You're the very first band. It's a great honor, so don't blow it!"

I laughed a fake laugh, then glanced over my shoulder at Julian and Danny. It was comforting to see that they looked as uptight as I'm sure I did. However, our new bass player, a guy named Waverly, didn't seemed phased by any of this. Trey had assured me he was a pro, and from the looks of it, he was.

"Just kidding," the voice continued. "You'll do great. This is what's going to happen. You'll be in total darkness, then, when you start the song, *BAM*! Lights and video! Music! The crowd goes nuts! Regina, I want you to count out the beat before you begin. One, two, three, four! Loud and clear for the light and video people. OK?" I nodded to the Wizard. "Great. Let's try this baby!"

The lights in the auditorium dimmed until I couldn't see a thing. I was aware of hushed and excited voices growing in volume in the wings of the stage. The Caverns were the new sensation, the new kids in town, so to speak, and from the sounds of it, we were attracting quite a bit of attention. That only served to make me even more nervous.

"Any time, Regina!" the Wizard boomed in the dark.

OK . . . OK! I thought, trying to steady myself. I took a deep breath, held it, then yelled, "One, two, three, four!" And then . . .

BAM!

A blinding barrage of white lights . . . psychedelic explosions of color on the massive screen behind us . . . amplified music loud enough to rocket us all the way up to the Shrine ceiling.

When all that sound and visual fury hit me, I felt as if I'd been plugged into a socket the size of say, the Caverns billboard on Sunset Boulevard. Amazing! Transporting! Mind-blowing!

The high-octane, unexpectedly powerful intro to "Hello, Goodbye" completely obliterated my nervousness. It was as if I had been lifted up by invisible hands and touched by the musical gods or something. OK, that's a bit over the top, but you get the idea. Anyway, after that, it was smooth sailing. The entire band went into one of those "zones." Julian and Danny and I were completely pumped, and our playing reflected that. Our new bass player was incredible, providing a power and oomph that Lorna had never been able to achieve.

So it was pure bliss playing and singing the rest of the song. More and more people filtered into the auditorium and crowded the wings of the stage to hear us. When we were singing, *"Hey-la, hey-hey-lo-ah"* over and over at the end of the song, I glanced over to see people in the wings of the stage—some of whom I'd grown up listening to on the radio and on CD—nodding and grooving in approval. *(They like us! They really, really like us!)* Then we hit the final chord.

CHEERS! APPLAUSE!

The bright lights and video screen snapped off when the song was over and we were once again illuminated by the normal stage lights. It felt like returning from a dream.

But the continuing applause was real enough, and then the Wizard said, "OK. That'll do," in a matter-of-fact, ironic way, which got a laugh from the backstage crowd. The next thing I knew, Trey was by my side and leading me triumphantly off the stage and into a cluster of famous smiling faces.

That didn't feel like a rehearsal, I thought as I was enveloped by the warm embrace of my musician peers. *It was more like a* coronation*!*

Yes, that's exactly what it felt like. A bowing down of the multitudes. An official "welcome to your new world."

20

"The Instigators . . . up next!" I was talking to Edge and Dr. Dre when I heard one of the headset people yell that as she walked past. I was mildly curious when I heard "the Instigators" called out. I had seen their poster at Amoeba, and now here they were at the Grammys. Who were these guys?

But seeing as I was talking to two musical legends, I wasn't about to excuse myself to go listen to some band I had never heard of. I mean, here Edge and Dr. Dre were talking to me as though I were their equal or something, and Dr. Dre was suggesting we should do something together in the future and I was gushing, "That would be great!" and feeling downright giddy from all the attention I was getting. Then I heard the opening line of the Instigators' song.

"I walk a lonely road / The only one that I have ever known / Don't know where it goes / But it's home to me and I walk alone."

I frowned and peeked around the curtain at the Instigators. Why were these guys up for a Grammy for singing a Green Day song? That's exactly the question I asked Edge and Dr. Dre. Their answer?

"Who's Green Day?"

What?! Say it again?! I didn't actually ask Edge and Dr. Dre to repeat what they had just said. I could tell from their expressions that they really, truly had never heard of Green Day before.

And that's when the fabric of my wish-come-true fantasy world split wide open. I felt as though everything around me suddenly dropped away, and I was hovering in a backstage black hole at the Shrine Auditorium. I think I grabbed on to a nearby curtain rope so that I wouldn't fall into the void.

The Instigators continued playing their song—or rather, Green Day's song—while I held tightly to the rope.

"I walk this empty street / On the boulevard of broken dreams / Where the city sleeps / And I'm the only one and I walk alone."

"Are you OK, Regina?" somebody asked me, but I didn't reply. Instead I slowly made my way toward the nearby stage wing so I could see this unknown band play "Boulevard of Broken Dreams," one of Green Day's biggest hits and certainly one of their most powerful songs.

Still in a total, haze-producing daze, I watched and listened until the Instigators front man sang, *"Sometimes I wish someone out there will find me / 'Til then, I walk alone."*

Then the song was over and the band walked offstage toward me. One by one they filed past. The lead singer was the last one. Instead of going by, he stopped right in front of me and smiled. "Hello, Regina Bloomsbury." I didn't say anything. "Rory," the lead singer said, holding out his hand. I shook it. Numbly. "You know what? We need to talk," Rory suggested. I nodded.

Numbly. "After we're done here, can I give you a lift to your hotel?" I nodded once again.

Numbly.

"Want anything to drink?"

I was in the back of Rory's limo, and the buildings of the University of Southern California were flashing by the tinted windows. We'd left the Shrine after I rehearsed my presentation of the Best Rap Album with Jay-Z and told Dad that I'd meet him and the rest of the band back at the hotel.

I shook my head no to Rory's offer of a drink. "So . . . where do we begin?" Rory smiled when he said this. He looked totally comfortable and relaxed. I studied him before I responded. Rory wasn't the best-looking guy in the world. With the right clothes and haircut, he managed to look pretty cool, but he wasn't what you'd call handsome. He was just a regular-looking guy, when you came right down to it.

"Why are you acting like you know me?" I finally asked. "And I don't mean because of my music or maybe you've seen me on MTV or anything like that."

Rory took a sip from his soda, then said, "We're living the same wish, Regina." I closed my eyes and pressed my fingers against my temples. *This, I cannot believe!*

"I know exactly how you're feeling right now. That's why I wanted to talk to you. To tell you that. After my wish was granted? I was thrown right into the thick of things and was all weirded out and had to figure everything out for myself. Same as you. Right? Then, on top of everything else, I catch some guy I never heard of one night on MTV singing his latest hit. Guess what it was."

Rory said this like an excited kid asking a friend to guess some fun secret. I shrugged. I didn't know and didn't want to guess and suddenly felt . . . betrayed by my Fairy Godmother.

"*'Blowin' in the Wind'*!" Rory announced with a laugh when I didn't answer. "Can you believe it? I had to tip my hat to the guy. Can you imagine trying to remember all the words to a bunch of Bob Dylan songs? But this dude did it. He's on a worldwide tour right now. I think he's in Europe."

Rory moved from his seat to sit next to me. It didn't feel aggressive or like he was putting the moves on me or anything like that. Rory felt more like an older brother. Or what I imagined having an older brother would feel like. "So I felt the same way you do right now, I'm sure. My wish wasn't, I don't know, private anymore after that, right? But it turned out to be just fine. 'Cause once I'd met the new Dylan? It was cool. The dude helped me adjust to all this. I had someone I could talk to. Relate to. Which was good, 'cause I don't know about your Wishmaster, but mine was totally scarce."

"Wishmaster?" I asked.

"The person who granted my wish. Whoever it was. Never met him. Or her. Don't really care to, at this point."

"I call mine my Fairy Godmother."

"Fairy Godmother. Wishmaster. Whatever. My point to you is this, Regina. You're still in the tryout phase, right?"

Tryout phase? I was disoriented and turned inside out by this new twist in my wish-come-true world and had to think about what Rory meant. "Oh . . . yeah. Tryout phase. Right. I'm in the tryout phase."

"Well, I don't know which way you're leaning, but you

gotta stay here! I guarantee it's everything you wished for, and more. I mean, c'mon. How cool was your rehearsal? You blew those people away! Even the hard-core, cynical old rock stars. Can you imagine anything better than that?"

I had to admit, I couldn't.

"You still look a bit out of it, Regina. I know this is a lot to lay on you. Let me get you something to drink."

"Just a . . . soda. Pepsi, if you got it."

"Your wish is my command!" Rory grabbed a Pepsi from the small fridge, popped it open, poured some into a glass, and handed it to me. After taking a sip, I did feel a little better. Especially when I put the cold glass against my hot head.

"So," I said after a bit. "Did you . . . well, did you have a hard time deciding whether to stay or not?"

Rory thought about that, like it was something that happened a very long time ago. "At first, maybe. Not much. I mean, yeah, there were those little pangs of guilt. About getting credit for all the Green Day songs. I'm sure you've felt that, huh?" I nodded, but realized that I'd been quite successful at burying that guilt over the past few days.

"Well, here's the other thing I wanted to tell you, Regina. It's really important. Are you listening?" Rory looked at me to make sure that I was. "It's OK. About the songs, I mean. It's essential you understand this. It's absolutely OK about the songs. For one thing, nobody's getting hurt here. The songs are still getting out there. The people still love them. So what if it's us instead of John or Paul or Billie Joe or Dylan? It's like . . . we're the guardians of this wonderful music."

Something occurred to me, for the first time. "Do they still exist? In this world? John, Paul, George, and Ringo? Billie Joe?"

"I wondered about that, too. A little while back, I almost went to Berkeley. To see if Billie Joe had become a short order cook or something. But then I realized, it just doesn't matter. It really doesn't. It's the songs that count. That should become your mantra. *It's the songs that count!*"

What Rory said made a kind of sense to me. And he said it so passionately. He seemed to really believe his mantra. It was comforting to hear that.

"By the way," Rory said, in an offhanded way. "We have the same manager."

What? "Get out," I said. "Trey?" Rory nodded. "You're kidding me."

"No, I'm not."

"He doesn't know about this, does he?"

"Yeah. He does."

I shook my head in dismay. Yet more complications. But wait a second. "Why didn't he say anything to me?"

"Probably waiting until after the Grammys. When you're here for good. But, yeah, Trey's just like us, actually. Made a wish to be the most successful manager in the world. Came true. So whoever comes through comes to him."

"Are you saying this happens a lot? People coming through?"

"Think about it, Regina. There are a lot of unhappy people out there who'd like to be somebody else."

What a sad thing to say. But Rory was probably right. As I thought about all of the unhappy people out there, Rory returned to his seat on the other side of the Hummer, stretched out on the seat, and put his hands behind his head. "Yeah . . . it definitely gets pretty wild here sometimes. The comings and goings, I mean. Just recently it looked like somebody was gonna be U2."

"U2? I was just talking to Edge at the Shrine."

"Yeah, they're back. This guy and his band were them for a week or so during his tryout phase, but then . . . I don't know, I guess he decided to return to his old life." Rory looked over at me and shook his head, as though that was the dumbest thing anyone could do. "Know what? You're for sure gonna win a couple of Grammys tomorrow. But you wanna bet on best song? I say I take it for 'Boulevard' over 'Yesterday.' Loser takes winner out to dinner." Rory held out his hand to shake on the bet.

I thought about that, then stood up—crouching over so my head didn't hit the ceiling—and reached over to shake Rory's hand. Nodding happily, Rory said, "Welcome to paradise, Regina."

PARADISE . . .

We were silent the rest of the way back to the Sheraton. Me sipping my Pepsi. Rory still stretched out on his seat, staring up at the ceiling, as though something were written up there. I couldn't tell if Rory liked what he was reading or not.

21

There were tons of messages for me when I got back to the hotel. Mom. Dad. Julian. Bradley. Trey.

Bradley wanted to let me know that I just had to come to the set that evening, around seven-ish. He was going to give me that surprise he had mentioned the first time we talked, when I was still back in Twin Oaks. That was an intriguing thing to ponder (what could it possibly be?), but I moved on to the other messages. Mom needed an outfit for the Grammys and wanted to know if I'd like to go shopping with her. Dad wanted to talk to me. So did Julian. As for Trey, all his message said was, "Trey. Call me."

I wasn't in the mood to talk to Trey, so I ignored his message. Mom wasn't in her room. Neither was Julian. Dad was. He asked if I'd like to go for a walk.

Sunset Boulevard, with its never-ending traffic and aggressive billboards, isn't exactly the best place for a stroll and a chat, so Dad asked Abernathy to take us somewhere nice and quiet. Abernathy pondered that for a moment, then drove us to a place called the Griffith Observatory, a cool-looking white building, with a '50s science-fictiony vibe and a white dome, that sits high on a hill overlooking the city.

It was nearing sunset when we got there. Dad was silent at first as we walked slowly around the observatory. He looked all bottled up, like he was going to burst with whatever was inside him. I figured I'd let him start the conversation. Eventually, he did.

"Your mom and I were a mismatch from the start, you know."

Whoa. Not what I was expecting. Especially considering that Dad never talked about Mom after she left. He took the divorce that hard. Still did. It was a while before he spoke again. "But . . . Laura was so different from anyone I'd ever known. Opposites attract and all that."

Uhhh, yeah. Since meeting Bradley, I kind of knew what Dad was talking about. I also knew that Mom and Dad had met one night at a gig that he was playing somewhere in Pennsylvania, but that's about all I knew about their relationship, and that had come from Mom, not Dad.

We stopped at a spot behind the observatory. The lights of L.A. were beginning their nightly twinkling display of restless energy.

"I don't want to make it sound like we never had any good times," Dad continued. "We did. At first. Mom loved it when the band was on the road. Even if it was just the bar circuit. She traveled with me every trip. It was after I stopped playing and took a teaching job that she got restless."

"So you should have never had me." The words just slipped out. But it seemed to be where this conversation was heading.

"Don't ever think that, Regina. You're the best thing that's ever happened to me. That's the God's truth." I didn't know what to say to that. But it felt good, hearing Dad say it. "As for your mom? I know she loves you. It might not have seemed that way to you sometimes these past years. But she was never the mothering type. It's not her fault. Just the way she is."

"Yeah, that's what she told me."

"She did?" Dad looked totally surprised.

"Just last night. The way she put it was, she's been waiting for me to grow up."

Dad actually smiled when he heard that. But then he got serious again. After a bit, he took a deep breath and exhaled slowly. I got the impression he was winding up to say something important.

"What I really wanted to talk to you about, Regina, was . . . when I saw you at the Shrine today? With Madonna and Edge and Taylor and all the others? Not to mention onstage. You looked so happy. You looked like . . . you were right where you belonged."

Wow. Another surprising statement from Dad.

"Hard as it is for me to say this, I can't expect you to leave all this and go back to Twin Oaks. I've been trying to keep things as normal as possible for you. I think that's important. But, if I'm honest, I want you home for selfish reasons as much as anything."

Selfish? What did that mean?

"If none of this had happened?" Dad explained. "If you were a normal high school kid? You'd be leaving home for college before I knew it, anyway. I wouldn't be trying to stop you from doing that. So why should I be trying to stop you from staying here in L.A.? That's what I've been asking myself. And the answer is, because I'll miss you when you're gone."

I felt like I could cry when Dad said that.

"So maybe it is time for you to go solo. I mean, yeah, of course I wish the whole Lorna thing hadn't happened. And all the bad feelings with the group. But I've played in enough bands to know that's par for the course. It's a rare band that gets along, believe me."

Looking at the ever-increasing lights of the city below, Dad and I were silent.

"So if you decide that you want to move here and buy a home and live with your mom? I'm not going to try to stop you anymore. And I promise I'll do everything I can to get along with Mom. I want to be welcome when I come to visit, after all."

Dad didn't say anything else after that. He had said what he had to say, and I could tell how hard it was for him. When I glanced sideways at him, I could see the red glow of the dying sun reflected in a tear that threatened to fall from his eye.

I quickly looked away. I didn't want to see my dad all emotional like that. Besides how bad it made me feel, I didn't want anything murking things up at that point. I had made my decision. I was staying in L.A. and that was that. Dad had even just given me his blessing.

But still, did things have to end this way? With me and Julian and me and Lorna fighting and everyone getting all worked up? And a tear that looked like a burst of fire in the corner of my dad's eye?

22

When Abernathy drove past the Starbucks near our hotel, I saw Julian sitting at a table near the window. I had a little time before heading off to the *P.C.H.* set, so after arriving at the Sheraton, I kissed Dad, told him I'd see him later, and walked to Starbucks.

I hesitated before going in. After my talk with Dad, I was wary of what might happen with Julian. But he had called me and wanted to talk about something, and I wasn't going to just ignore him.

Like the last time, Julian was immersed in his notebook and didn't see me walk across the coffee shop toward his table.

"Hi," I said when I arrived, but didn't sit down.

"Oh . . . yeah. Hi." Julian looked disoriented. Like he didn't know where he was.

I couldn't help but laugh. "I don't know how you do this, Julian." He gave me a perplexed look. "Work on songs in a place like this. I need total silence."

Julian nodded. For some reason, he looked like I'd just

given him a problem to solve instead of commenting on his work habits.

"Want to sit down?" he finally asked. "I called you back after you'd called me back, but you weren't in your room."

I sat. Julian stared at his notebook, then closed it. He looked nervous. Well, not nervous, exactly, but something was going on in that head of his.

"What did you want to talk about?" I asked.

Julian didn't answer right away. It was like he'd forgotten what he had called me about. "Well, here's the thing, Regina. This has been such a crazy week, you know?" I nodded. "I mean . . ." Julian laughed suddenly.

"What?"

"I don't know where to start, really. Your amnesia. Your catfight with Lorna. The Grammy rehearsal. Was that intense, or what?"

"Which? The Grammy rehearsal or my fight with Lorna?"

"Both. But I was referring to the Grammy rehearsal."

"It was intense," I agreed.

"All the concerts we've played didn't even come close. I don't know about you, but I felt like . . . a real rock star up there."

"Yeah. Me, too."

"But at the same time . . ."

Silence.

"I'm listening, Julian."

"Well, I felt uncomfortable up there. On the Shrine stage."

"Why?"

"Because I feel like I'm riding on your coattails."

"That's ridiculous."

"It's not. I've been feeling that way for a while now. That's what I wanted to tell you. I've been thinking about this a lot, and I want you to know it's OK with me if you go your own way. It'll force me to concentrate on my own stuff. And that's a good thing. I've been needing a good kick in the butt."

What's going on here? I thought. *First Dad. Now Julian. It's like they're both opening the door for me and saying, "Go! Leave us! It's OK."* I couldn't figure out why they'd changed all of a sudden.

I guess Julian saw that I was kind of perplexed, because then he said, "I just don't want to fight anymore, you know? I mean, I feel really bad about yesterday. All you did was offer to help with my lyrics, and I was a total shit about it. If I'm honest, Regina? I've just been jealous, that's all. So is Lorna. It's hard being around someone so talented. Someone who grabs all the heat."

I stared at my hot chocolate. Julian made me uncomfortable, talking about how talented I was.

"So . . . we'll do the Grammys. We'll do the tour next year. Then you strike out on your own. I'll strike out on mine."

I admired Julian for his guts and courage. That's what it takes, after all, to put yourself out there, creatively speaking.

"Julian?" There was something I was wondering about. *Don't ask this question*, part of me warned. But a bigger part of me needed to know.

"What?"

"I told you the truth about my amnesia." Julian studied me, waiting for my question. "I guess what I'm wondering is, when we were together? How was it?" Julian pushed back a lock of his unruly hair. He shifted in his seat. He avoided looking at me. "I'm sorry. It's not a fair question."

"It was good," Julian said suddenly. Then he looked me right in the eye. "No, it was great, Regina. But hey, it wasn't meant to be, right? I shouldn't have said that about Bradley. Him getting his hooks in you and all that. He seems like an OK guy. Sort of."

I stared out the window at a street musician a little ways down the street, playing an oboe. I needed to focus on something other than Julian for a minute so I could compose myself. *I told you this was dangerous territory.* And it really was. Like seeing my dad cry, thinking about Julian and me together made things murky.

Murky. Not good.

Clarity. Good.

Since making my decision not to go back to Twin Oaks, I'd achieved clarity. *So just keep things with Julian strictly professional,* I told myself.

"Can I see your song?" I asked.

Julian considered my request, then opened his notebook to the proper page and slid it across the table to me. As I read the lyrics to his new song, I could sense Julian fidgeting in his seat. As it turned out, he didn't need to get all uptight.

"They're very good lyrics, Julian." I wasn't just saying that, either. They were personal and dealt with being an artist and how vulnerable that makes you feel but how you can't help choosing the creative life. It chooses you.

"You really think so?" Julian asked tentatively. It was like he didn't believe me. Julian's response made me wonder if creative people ever get over their insecurity.

"Yes, I do think so. They're different and original and personal. You were right. You don't need my help."

"I didn't really mean that, Regina. If you have any suggestions . . ."

I studied the lyrics again, then said, "I don't. You nailed it." Julian smiled. He could tell that I meant it. I suddenly noticed the clock on the wall over Julian's shoulder. "Gosh. I have to go."

"Tell Bradley I said hi."

There was no malice or sarcasm in Julian's voice when he said that. "I will." I slid Julian's notebook back to him. "Going back to the hotel?"

"No, Hayley's meeting me here in a few."

"Tell her I said hi." I was hoping there wasn't any sarcasm in my voice when I said that.

"I will," Julian said.

"So . . . see you tomorrow."

"At the Grammys. Where a good time will be had by all."

I smiled, gave Julian a wave, and headed for the exit. I got out of there just in time. If I'd stayed just a moment longer, Julian might have seen that it was *my* turn to cry. Which I definitely didn't want him to see. I wiped a tear away as I walked past the oboe player. Then I stopped, retraced my steps, took out a hundred-dollar bill, and dropped it in his case.

23

"There she is!"

Andy, the second AD, gave me a big grin and a high five when he saw me outside the Warner Brothers soundstage, where they film the interior scenes of *P.C.H.*

"*Andy*," I replied pointedly.

"You remembered!" Andy seemed genuinely pleased. "Brad's in his trailer. Just around the corner." Andy walked off, chatting into his headset, which made him look like he was talking to himself.

I have to say, there's a real buzz on a film set. And a buzz is just what I needed to take my mind off being with Dad and Julian and all of the emotions that were stirred up as a result of talking to them. When I found Bradley in his trailer, he pushed aside all of the script rewrites on his couch to make space for me to sit.

"So what's with this surprise?" I asked as soon as I had settled in next to him.

"Before we get to that . . . you were great on the *Tonight Show* last night."

"Thanks. What's the surprise?"

Bradley just smiled.

"C'mon, Bradley."

"It's a good one."

"OK. What is it?"

Bradley raised his eyebrows mysteriously.

"Don't do this to me," I pleaded.

Finally, Bradley relented and said, "Ready for your close-up?"

What Bradley meant by "close-up" was me, acting in a scene with him, on the number-one-rated teen show on television. He had talked to the producer and director the week before, and they thought it would be terrific if I'd do it. With all the press about Bradley and me, I guess they figured, cool! Why not?

I surprised myself by how quickly I said yes to the cameo. I mean, a few days before? No way would I have done it. But I'd grown a little, confidence-wise, since arriving in L.A. So that felt kind of good.

Turns out there was lots to do to get me ready for my big scene. Andy took me to the wardrobe trailer and introduced me to Stacy. She made it clear that she was the costume *designer*, as opposed to one of the set costumers, who worked *under* her. She was pretty intense and serious about creating the totally new, this-is-what-the-teens-will-be-wearing-after-they-see-the-fashions-on-our-show outfits.

I wasn't sure that I liked my fashion rags of the near future after I'd been fitted in them. They were kind of tarty and nothing like I'd ever worn in real life. *You're just role-playing, Regina.* That's what I reminded myself. Besides, it felt like I was dressing up for Halloween or something.

After my wardrobe fitting, Andy escorted me to the hair/makeup trailer. It's difficult not to feel like a star when you're coddled and cooed over while sitting in a makeup chair, let me tell you. I'd had a taste of that while we were making the video, but this was first class in comparison.

Charlene, the makeup person—who looked like she could be a model or actress herself—and Lawrence—the hair-stylist, who looked like he would be right at home on one of those reality top-model runway shows (OK, I'll admit I watch them from time to time)—descended on me like I was a famous rock star or something. (Oh, that's right. I was!)

"Nice cheekbones."

"The hair's all wrong. Sorry, darling, but it is!"

"We'll cover that blemish, no problem." (What can I say? Even rock stars get zits.)

"Very pretty eyes."

It was whirlwind makeover time, the end result being a strange-looking person staring back at me from the mirror. I mean, really. Who was that girl? The clothes, hair, and makeup had transformed me into an alternate version of myself. Scrap alternate version. "Myself" had totally disappeared into the "mirror" Regina, with her heavy blush makeup, raccoon eyes, and new-style do. The girl in the mirror was so different from how I normally looked that I didn't know how to process it. Halloween, indeed!

Andy returned to the trailer after about a half hour and announced I was "needed on set." It was time for . . .

Lights!
Cameras!
Action!

Well, not much action. Not at first, anyway. For the next three hours I stood around on the soundstage, waiting for them to finish the scene before mine, which took place in a fake classroom. After that, I was led to a fake version of a high school hallway, the setting for my scene with Bradley.

The director, who was the same person I'd seen on the beach, was a rail-thin, hyper kinda guy who looked to be somewhere in his thirties. He introduced himself, told me how thrilled everyone was to have me on *P.C.H.*, then explained the scene that I was going to be in.

Bradley and I would be at his locker, talking between classes. I was supposed to act like I was totally in love with him. Melissa would then appear out of the crowd of students in the hallway and walk up to us. After giving me a look that could kill, Melissa would slam Bradley's locker shut, take him by the arm, and lead him off down the hall.

That's when I had my big line. "I'll see you in geography, Zane!" The director told me to say the line like my entire life depended on seeing Zane in geography. I nodded and kinda frowned to show that I was really serious about all this as the director explained the scene to me.

After that, it was time for rehearsal. We ran through the

scene a couple times, then we had to wait for half an hour or so for the lighting crew to set up the lights for the scene. Two girls and a guy—stand-ins—took our places by the locker so the cameraman could see how the light would look on our faces.

I was really nervous as I waited to do the scene. Bradley and Melissa were the total opposite, joking and talking about the upcoming weekend. When we were told everything was ready, Bradley took me by the hand and led me down the fake school hallway to the locker.

"You're gonna do just great," he said with a smile as the extras took their places in the hallway and the first AD told everyone to be quiet. When the cameraman took his place behind the camera, and the director said, "Let's shoot the rehearsal."

We wound up shooting a lot more than the rehearsal. I was glad, too, because I totally stunk the first few times around, to be honest. Which is probably why we had to do the scene so many times to get it right. The director didn't say that, he was very encouraging, but that's the impression I got.

I knew it was my nervousness that was making my one line sound so stilted, so unnatural. I was surprised at how nervous I actually was. I'd already acted in the music video, after all, and played on the Shrine stage, for gosh sakes. But this was different from both of those things. In the music video, I had "acted naturally," as Ringo once sang. I was just being myself. On the Shrine stage, I was playing a song I knew by heart.

Here, I was playing a character. A total airhead is what I

was playing. Besides that, there were all these silhouettes of people moving back and forth behind the bright, hot lights, and then there was the sudden call for "Silence!" and suddenly it was deathly quiet and then it was "Action!" and then you were supposed to act as though you really were standing in a high school hallway and it was daytime, not night as you knew it really was outside. It gave me a new appreciation for actors, that's for sure.

Bradley was really sweet about it all. He complimented me after each take, told me I was doing great even though I knew I wasn't, especially when I called him Bradley a couple times instead of Zane. But by the last take, I had finally relaxed and was even starting to enjoy myself.

When the first AD announced, "That's a wrap!" Bradley totally embarrassed me by leading a round of applause for my "film debut." Then, in front of the entire crew of *P.C.H.*, he gave me a kiss.

There was a big "whoo-hoooo!" from the people on set when Bradley kissed me. Then cast members started coming up and congratulating me on my scene, and Melissa invited Bradley and me back to her trailer for a little wrap party. And that's when those seven little words popped up yet one more time. (Third time the charm?)

A girl could get used to this.

I noticed something when I was with Bradley and Melissa and some of the other *P.C.H.* actors in Melissa's trailer. They were all a little older than I was—not by much, a few years maybe—but they seemed to be light-years more worldly.

More sophisticated. It was how they expressed themselves. What they talked about. I felt like a kid among adults.

So I kept kind of quiet, but nobody seemed to mind because everyone was loud and talking over each other, and they were all pretty hyped up. I figured that was because it was the end of a long week of filming. Sort of like getting out of school on Friday. It was that kind of manic energy.

Only the *P.C.H.* people talked about maybe flying up to Tahoe for a bit of skiing or maybe going to Vegas and catching a show. Heck, I was happy to go sledding at a place in Twin Oaks called the Arboretum. That was my idea of a fun weekend in February. Assuming there was snow, of course.

Anyway, after a while, I said good night to everyone, and Bradley walked me to my limo. Bradley looked kind of down all of a sudden. It was the first time I'd seen him like that.

"What's wrong?" I asked.

"Nothin'."

"Yes, there is."

Bradley looked hesitant to say anything.

"You can tell me anything, Bradley. You know that."

After a moment, Bradley said, "Melissa just told me she got a movie."

"What?"

"Melissa. She's doing a movie on our hiatus."

"Well, that's great, right? Now you're both doing a movie on hiatus." Bradley had told me about his movie when we were in the cemetery.

"Yeah, but hers has a bigger budget."

I couldn't believe what Bradley had just said, it was so ridiculous. "You're not telling me you're upset because Melissa's movie has a bigger budget than yours, are you?"

"C'mon, Regina. You know how competitive it is out here. You're competitive with other bands, right?"

I thought about the Circuit Club and how they were going to snatch Danny and Lorna away from the Caverns and how I had tried to persuade Mrs. Densby to give the Caverns the Back to School gig instead of letting DJ Jimmy do it. That was being kind of competitive, I guess. Still . . .

"Melissa's your friend, though, Bradley. She's on the same show as you. I'd think you'd be happy for her."

"I read this quote once," Bradley replied. "It was by a famous writer or something. He said . . ." Bradley took a moment to recall the quote. " 'It is not enough to succeed. Others must fail.' "

"Ouch. That's rather stringent."

"That's rather L.A., Regina."

As I thought about that, Bradley's face suddenly brightened. "Melissa doesn't have tomorrow to look forward to, though, does she?"

Tomorrow? What was tomorrow?

"I'll see you at the Grammys, girl."

Oh, right. I had gotten Bradley a backstage pass, which he was really excited about.

"I'll see *you* in geography," I said, then smiled. I guess Bradley didn't think that was very funny, or maybe he didn't get it right away, 'cause he just looked at me, deadpan. But then he kind of chuckled.

"I better get going," I said, then I gave Bradley a quick kiss and hopped into the Hummer. As Abernathy drove off, I looked back. Bradley was still standing in the darkness by the soundstage. Then the Hummer took a left turn, and I couldn't see him anymore.

24

Sitting in the back of the Hummer on the way to the hotel, I found myself thinking about the strange conversation I just had with Bradley. But I shook off the thought and tried to concentrate, for the first time, really, about all the things that needed to be done after Dad and Julian and Danny left on Sunday. (Lorna had already gone home.)

First thing, of course, was Mom and I had to deal with the Beverly Hills place. I wasn't sure what all you needed to do to buy a house, but I was pretty sure it wasn't as simple as just handing over a bunch of money.

Second, the house was ridiculously huge, so we'd have to get all kinds of furniture for it.

Then, by the time Mom and I got settled into our new digs, I'd probably have to go on tour with the Caverns.

After that, it would be time to start recording my solo album. I was looking forward to figuring out what Beatles/Bloomsbury songs were going to be on it.

All the while, I'd be hanging out with Bradley and the *P.C.H.* people and Rory from the Instigators and who knew who else?

Incredible! It was still hard to believe all this was actually going to happen. Before my tipping point, I was just playing a fantasy game. And trying to have some fun. But now . . . this was what I'd truly wished for. A busy, exciting, never-a-dull-moment life!

I was in the midst of my mental musings when the limo passed the Hollywood Bowl. The sight of the H.B. sign stirred something in me. Something powerful. Something important.

But I was too caught up planning my future to put my finger on what it was. As the sign disappeared from my field of vision, the divider between the front and back seats of the limo slid silently into its slot.

"You OK?" Abernathy asked, looking at me in his rearview mirror.

"Sure. Do I look OK?"

"I guess. It's good to see you smile again, that's for sure. Considering what happened back there on the floor yesterday."

"Yeah. Sorry about that."

"It's not the first time there's been a fight in my limo. Won't be the last, I'm afraid." Abernathy left the divider down but was silent as he continued down Highland Boulevard. I think he was being polite, not putting the divider back up. That way if I wanted to continue the conversation, I could. Which I did.

"Abernathy?"

"Mmhmmm."

"How long have you been driving a limo?"

"About ten years."

"Must have seen a lot of stuff over those years. Driving celebrities around."

"The good, the bad, and the ugly. Some I've driven when they first got to L.A. Wide-eyed and innocent as babes, they usually are. Then I've driven them after they've made it."

"You mean, like me?"

Abernathy frowned. "No, I didn't drive you when you first came to L.A."

Woops. I should have known that. "So . . . do these celebrities change much?" I asked, anxious to deflect attention from my latest slipup.

Abernathy studied me in the mirror. He looked as if he were wondering why I had asked the question. His answer was slow and cautious. "From what I've seen, Regina, fame is kind of like a tidal wave. You might see it coming, sense it coming, but there's not much you can do to avoid getting swept up in it. It's just too powerful."

"Are you saying these people get stuck-up?" Some of the *P.C.H.* people struck me as being that way, actually.

Before Abernathy answered, we stopped at a red light next to a bus that was totally painted—back to front, top to bottom—with an advertisement for *Meet the Caverns!* It gave me a bit of a start. I'd never seen a bus "wrapped" like that back home.

"I think what it is, is some of these people come to think of themselves as the center of the universe," Abernathy said as the bus drove off, spouting exhaust in its wake and obscuring the Caverns' larger-than-life faces in a black fog. "And they're not, of course. Nobody is."

Abernathy's statement hung in the air as he drove the rest of the way to the Sheraton. He guided the limo into the circular driveway, got out, and opened the door for me. As I slid out of the backseat, he reached into his pocket and pulled out a business card. Handing it to me, he said, "I'm off for the night. But if you need me for anything, don't hesitate to call. OK?"

"Thanks, Abernathy." Abernathy tipped his hat and got back into the car. I waved good-bye, then walked to the revolving door and pushed through it. When I got to my room, I checked my messages.

"Why didn't you call?" (Trey.)

"Sorry I missed your call. I'll be at Starbucks until they kick me out." (Julian, before I saw him at Starbucks.)

"You missed out, girl. Great shopping trip! See you tomorrow!" (Mom.)

"Have you listened to my CD? Good luck at the Grammys!" (Stuart, the kid in the stairway.)

"Hi, I'm driving home. Just wanted to say you did great tonight, Regina. Everyone on *P.C.H.* loves you. By the way, so do I. Sweet dreams!" (Bradley.)

I smiled at the last message. Bradley actually said he loved me!

Heading across the room, I slowly peeled off my clothes and threw them on the floor. Entering the bathroom, I laughed when I saw myself in the mirror. I'd handed in my *P.C.H.* outfit after filming was over but forgot that I still wore my Halloween face and hair.

"Look at you!" I said, pointing in delight at my mirror

image. But my smile quickly faded. When I was wearing my tarty clothes, it all went together. It was a costume. But I was down to my tank top and underwear, and my makeup and hair looked absurd. Scary, really.

So I stripped the rest of the way and jumped into the shower and washed off all my makeup and the gel out of my hair. When I emerged from the shower, I looked like a *baby*. Seriously. Naked. No makeup. Just me. The original Regina.

The original Regina . . .

What did I think about her at that point in my wish-world journey? To be honest, I thought she was kind of naive and old-fashioned and just so totally out of it, as far as being in the real world was concerned. It was clear to me that it was time to say good-bye to the original Regina, time to leave her behind.

But I couldn't. Not just yet.

I stood for a while, looking in the mirror, and that kicked off all kinds of thoughts—moving to L.A. and Julian and Bradley and Dad and Mom and the Instigators' Rory—then I got tired of thinking so much, so I turned away from myself, put on the fluffy white bathrobe that hung on a hook on the bathroom door, and slapped off the bathroom light on my way out.

I sat on the sofa and watched a bit of TV after my shower. I was pretty tired from another long, intense day, but I needed to unwind, so I clipped my toenails and watched the end of *Pretty in Pink*, which was playing on TCM or one of those channels.

"Why are you going back to that guy?" I yelled at Molly as

she and Andy what's-his-name stared moonily at each other in the hall after Molly left the prom. I'd seen the movie several times, and it always bugged me that Molly couldn't figure out that she and Ducky belonged together. It ruined the whole movie for me, that ending.

I turned off the TV when the credits came on and got into bed. "Well, Regina?" I called out in the dark to my Regina Beatle doll on the nightstand. "Ready for our big day tomorrow? It's gonna be the first day of the rest of our lives!"

The Regina doll looked as ready as she'd ever be. But was I? Was I *absolutely* ready to accept those Grammys and leave my old world behind?

What's with you, Regina? I scolded myself. *Of course you're ready. You've made your decision. Onward and upward!*

I rolled over, pulled up my covers, and quickly nodded off. Ah, but that did not mean I was about to have a good, restful night's sleep.

Quite the opposite, actually. There would be another one of those very real IMAX-type dreams. And a nocturnal visit to one of L.A.'s most famous places. And an absolutely surreal experience that would make the past few days look like kids' stuff.

25

I have to explain about "Saturday Night at the Movies" before I get into my night-before-the-Grammys dream.

I was about seven or eight when Dad jump-started our weekly movie event. On that appointed day, Dad would rent two movies, and he and Mom and me would settle in for a double feature. Dad wanted us to have SNATM because that's what his family had done when he was a kid. Only they went to the Echo or Colonial Drive-In theaters. That was back in the day, before all the drive-in movies were closed down.

I remember Dad telling me how much he loved those nights at the Colonial and Echo, mainly for the movies but also because it was one of the few times his entire family was together. So he wanted to re-create that for me.

It worked. Like Dad, I loved my version of Saturday Night at the Movies. So much so that he and I kept it going even after Mom left. I think it became even more special after that. More necessary. When I hit my teens, though, our private movie club was disbanded. After all, what self-respecting teen wants to stay at home on Saturday night, watching a movie with her dad? But for a period of about four or five years, it was great.

So anyway, Saturday Night at the Movies is where I was in my night-before-the-Grammys L.A. dream. Sprawled on the sofa in my Twin Oaks living room, watching *Help!*, the Beatles' second film.

Dad's on one side of me. Mom's on the other. We each have our own bowls of popcorn. I'm a little girl.

Then, suddenly . . .

The TV, as though responding to the snap of a magician's fingers, does a very strange thing. Images from my L.A. journey—and the people populating that journey—replace *Help!* and begin flickering on the screen, one after another.

L.A. from the air.
Dad.
Julian.
The Caverns' Sunset Strip billboard.
Abernathy.
Bradley.
The Beverly Hills home with the guitar-shaped pool.
Mom.
Trey.
The Grammy rehearsal at the Shrine.
Lorna.
Chris Rock.
The Hollywood Bowl.
Rory.
Danny.

Some of the images return, over and over. Some don't. Confused, I look to my parents for some explanation. But . . .

They've disappeared! I'm all alone on the sofa!

I've never felt so alone in my whole life.

The images suddenly speed up and become a mesmerizing blur. I'm hypnotized, looking at them. I forget about how lonely I am. Like the whirring pictures on a slot machine, they begin to slow down.

I'm glued to the TV screen, anxious and excited and somehow knowing that the final image on the screen will be very important.

Slower . . .

and . . .

slowwwwwer . . .

the images . . .

tick . . .

by . . .

until . . .

finally . . .

JACKPOT!

The final image!

Wait . . . what?

What does *that* mean?

My eight-year-old self sits on the sofa, staring at the TV with a frown, disappointed and confused. She has no idea what the final image on the screen is supposed to mean.

...

But *I* did. When I jolted awake with the image of the Hollywood Bowl in my head, I knew exactly what it meant.

Passing the Bowl earlier had stirred something in me, but I
was too busy imagining my famous future to really care what
that something was. Now, as I lay in bed and stared at the
ceiling, I was amazed that I had burrowed so far into my
wish-come-true world that I hadn't immediately responded to
the sight of the famous Bowl sign.

What's so important about the Bowl?

The Beatles played two historic concerts there, in 1964 and
1965. I know that because I have the album, *Live at the Hollywood Bowl.* Or, rather, used to have it. Like Shea Stadium
and the Cavern Club, the Bowl is hallowed ground in the Beatles universe.

So the thing I knew when I woke up from my Saturday
Night at the Movies dream was, I had to go to the Bowl. Right
then. At that moment. At . . . (a glance at the digital bedside
clock) 3:39 a.m.!

Did you ever see *Field of Dreams*? That was one of Dad's
SNATM selections. Kind of a guy flick, but I liked it just the
same. (Mom didn't.)

Anyway, in *Field of Dreams*, this farmer-type guy is out in
his cornfield and suddenly he hears this voice that says, "If
you build it, he will come." Then he sees a vision of a baseball
field in the middle of his cornfield. Just like that, he knows he
has to build a baseball field in the middle of his cornfield.
He just *knows* it, and he also knows that something very

important will happen if he does. He just doesn't know what that something is.

That's how it was with me. When I woke up with that image of the Hollywood Bowl in my head, I just knew I had to go there. And if I did, something important would happen.

Something else I was pretty certain of when I got out of bed and started to get dressed: My Fairy Godmother had sent me that dream. I hadn't tried to make contact with her since I'd arrived in L.A., but now I really wanted to. So I turned on my computer and logged on to www.wish-come-true.uni. Turns out all I had to do was click on the wishing well and up came a blank e-mail page, waiting for me to type in a message.

I typed, "Why do you want me to go to the Hollywood Bowl?"

I thought that was pretty clever. If she responded, I'd know that she had sent me the dream. If she didn't write back, I was going anyway.

There was no immediate reply, so I finished getting dressed, splashed some water on my face, and was putting on my jacket when . . .

Bling!

Fairy Godmother e-mail! It read:

You figure it out, Regina. I can't do all the work for you.

What a sassy F.G.! At least, I knew I was right. Which meant going to the Bowl in the middle of the night wasn't as crazy an idea as I might have thought. But what was going to happen there?

Only one way to find out.

26

"Abernathy? It's Regina."

Abernathy grunted a hello. I had considered calling a cab, but I didn't want some anonymous guy driving me to the Bowl. Not at four a.m. But I did feel bad about waking Abernathy. "I'm sorry about the time, but you said I could call whenever I needed you. And I kinda need you."

"Be there in fifteen minutes."

Abernathy hung up. I couldn't tell if he was upset or not about me waking him, so I went downstairs right away so he wouldn't have to wait for me when he got to the hotel.

I was standing outside the Sheraton, looking up and down the quiet Strip, when the white Hummer appeared. Abernathy pulled up to the curb in front of me. I opened the front passenger door and hopped inside.

Abernathy's face was blank. A mask. I couldn't tell how he was feeling. "Where to, young lady?" Even his voice, normally so expressive, was flat, indecipherable.

"Are you OK, Abernathy?"

"Just tired."

"Sorry about that. I really appreciate . . ."

Abernathy interrupted my sentence by raising his eyebrows, his expression asking the same question he had already asked. *Where to, young lady?*

"The Hollywood Bowl."

Abernathy responded to that with a deadpan expression. Then he drove through the hotel's circular driveway and pointed the limo down Sunset toward Highland Avenue. After a few blocks, Abernathy asked, "What's at the Hollywood Bowl?"

I thought carefully about my answer. Then I admitted, "I don't know." Abernathy pursed his lips. He was perplexed, of course. "I'm sorry, Abernathy. I just know I have to go there."

Abernathy didn't say anything the rest of the way. Neither did I. It felt exciting and dangerous and clandestine, being out so late. Sunset Boulevard was pretty much deserted. I saw a few homeless people on the sidewalks, hunkered down for the night. I felt bad for them, of course. And weird, too. Here I was, in a mile-long Hummer. So I looked at them out of the corner of my eye, feeling embarrassed about traveling in such luxury.

But then we were heading up Highland, and my stomach started to jump and squirm the closer we got to the Bowl. When Abernathy approached the Bowl driveway, he put on his turn signal. That must have been a habit, putting on that signal, because there was absolutely no traffic.

After turning into the driveway, Abernathy drove a little ways before he was stopped by a security guard who sat next to a chain stretched across the driveway. It seemed kind of odd to me, a security guard at the Bowl in the middle of the night, especially considering that it was off-season. There weren't any concerts scheduled for at least a couple of months.

"She wants to do *what?*" the guard said after Abernathy had explained why we had come to the Bowl. The guard, whose head looked too big for his rather smallish body, stared at me with a comically quizzical expression on his rubbery face.

"Just sit in the stands for a while," I replied, in what I hoped was an innocent-enough tone.

The guard looked at Abernathy, his expression asking, *Is this girl nuts?* Abernathy returned the silent communication, raising his eyebrows in a way that said, *What could it hurt?*

The guard thought about my unusual request for quite a while. He looked me up and down. Gave Abernathy another quizzical look. Finally, he said, "You owe me, Abe," and removed the chain.

Abernathy, who I figured knew the guard from all of the times he'd driven people to the Bowl, saluted his friend and drove the limo slowly up a wide, concrete area that bordered one side of the Bowl.

Suddenly, there it was. I got a tingling sensation right down my spine when I saw the famous half dome rising up in the dark. It looked like some kind of ancient monument. A Stonehenge of the musical universe.

Abernathy parked the limo next to a hill covered by ever-green trees. He pointed to an area just to the right of the Bowl dome. "Hop over those turnstiles, walk up that ramp, take a left, and you're there."

"Thanks, Abernathy." I felt a sudden urge to kiss him before getting out, so I gave him a quick peck on the cheek.

"*Go*, will you," he said, but his annoyed dismissal couldn't hide the fact that he seemed pleased with my show of affection.

I approached a turnstile and jumped over it. A sudden breeze blew through the trees, creating a mysterious whispering sound, a fitting sound track for my nocturnal visit. I walked toward the steep concrete ramp Abernathy had pointed out. To my right, a hill rose sharply. To my left was a high hedge that blocked any view of the Bowl. I walked up the ramp until I arrived at the first of several entrances to the amphitheater.

I stopped before going in. Why was I here, again? What did I think was going to happen? I felt silly all of a sudden. *You're at the Hollywood Bowl in the middle of the night, Regina! What is wrong with you?!*

I reminded myself that my F.G. had sent me here. *Have faith, girl.* So I took a deep breath, walked on through the break in the high hedge, and . . .

There it was. The Bowl.

Maybe it was because it was the middle of the night and no one was there. Maybe the musical ghosts of all the performers who had played there hung around at this hour. Or maybe it was the almost-full moon, hanging up there in a cloudless sky, illuminating everything with its gorgeous, soft light. Whatever it was, the sight of the Bowl actually took my breath away.

The place looked beautiful in its simplicity. The seats,

curved wooden bleachers for the most part, rose steeply in a slowly widening V shape. The silhouettes of pine trees, at the top and on one side of the amphitheater, defined and emphasized its shape. That shape naturally pointed to the stage, with its extremely cool-looking, distinctive half-circle shell.

I smiled at the sight in front of me. Even if nothing else happened, even if I was wrong about coming to the Bowl, just being at the place and absorbing the wonderful vibes would have made the trip worthwhile.

After imprinting the sights and sounds and smells of the place on my brain for a few minutes, I walked slowly along a wide aisle that separated one section of the Bowl from another, higher-up section. I turned at the first set of concrete stairs and climbed up the steep incline until I was about halfway up the amphitheater. I chose a wooden bleacher seat and sat down. I couldn't help but grin as I gazed at the stage.

The Beatles had been here! It wasn't difficult to picture them playing on those two warm August evenings almost fifty years ago.

For one thing, I had read about the two concerts in a book called *Ticket to Ride*, written by a reporter who was there. This reporter recalled how much the Beatles enjoyed those concerts (something they were beginning not to do) largely because they could actually hear themselves play. Usually, they couldn't hear themselves because the sound systems were pretty bad back then (the Bowl's was very good, apparently) and their fans screamed too loud. So they gave spirited performances those two nights, which you can tell from their *Live at the Hollywood Bowl* album.

So, yeah, between that book and the album and the tons of pictures and film footage of Beatlemania I'd seen, it was real easy to imagine what it must have been like, on those nights, being right in the thick of things.

But then, something incredible happened. I still can't believe it, even now as I write this. But it did. It totally did. So hold on tight. 'Cause you know what?

It's time for . . .

27

"JOHHHHNNN!!!!"
"PAAUULLLLLL!!!!!!!"
"GEORRRRRGE!!!!!!"
"RINGOOOOOO!!!!!"

Sitting shock-still, I stared in stunned surprise at the wall of girls who had appeared from out of nowhere and now surrounded me, a crying, screaming, leaping, grabbing-their-hair-and-reaching-out-toward-the-stage mass of human frenzy.

I was dumbfounded. I couldn't believe what I was seeing. One moment I had been all alone in the Hollywood Bowl, the next . . . here I was.

At a Beatles Hollywood Bowl concert!

I was so blown away by my instantaneous trip through space and time that I hardly moved for what must have been several minutes. I remember reaching out at one point and touching the girl who stood in front of me. (Everyone was standing but me.) My hand didn't go right through her, like I kind of expected. The girl was real.

The wild tribal energy that throbbed around me eventually pulled me out of my stupefied state. That and the music.

The music.

It was unlike anything I had ever heard. I've spent tons of hours listening to music. I've been to a lot of concerts. But nothing prepared me for this.

The music was so . . . immediate. So raw. So primal. It was like getting hit right in the gut. In a good way.

"Well, she looked at me / And I, I could see / That before too long, I'd fall in love with her . . ."

"I Saw Her Standing There."

Paul was singing "I Saw Her Standing There"! And all I had to do was stand on my seat, and I'd be able to see him.

So that's what I did.

Carefully, slowly, I stood up. And let me tell you, when I stood on my seat and saw the Beatles on the stage of the Hollywood Bowl, I almost keeled over. Seriously. I had to grab on to the girl in front of me to prevent myself from falling.

I mean, there they were!

There was *John*, rooted to the stage in that cool, slightly bowlegged stance of his.

There was *Paul*, more animated than his writing partner, smiling and flirting with the crowd as though we were all one big, beautiful woman.

There was *George*, standing between Paul and John, looking somewhat amused by all the frenzy as he played his guitar and sang harmony with Paul.

There was *Ringo*, high up on a platform behind his bandmates, moving his head back and forth in that cute way of his as he smiled at the sea of people who rose up in front of him.

So, OK. Now I'm standing on my seat. Staring at the Beatles. But I still can't quite believe what I'm seeing. I'm just a spectator, staring openmouthed like an idiot at the sight in front of me. I was part of the scene, but not *in* it, if you know what I mean.

Until the girl next to me whacked me in the head when she lost her footing, tumbled off her seat, and sprawled on the concrete at my feet.

I'll be forever grateful to that girl, whoever she was. That sharp slap to my skull was like a cattle-prod-crack to my brain.

Snap out of it, Regina! the blow announced. *You're here. Don't think about it. Just enjoy!*

Before I knew what I was doing, my head started to bob in time to the music. My body started moving. I began to feel very, very warm. Then hot.

It was a totally weird sensation, let me tell you. I felt like I was suddenly possessed. Not quite in control of myself.

What on earth is going on here? I wondered.

Well, that was obvious. One simple word described what I was feeling.

BEATLEMANIA!!!

But hold on. There was one last thing I had to do to join the club. And I did it.

I screamed!

I'd never screamed at a concert before. But after that first primal blast, I never let up. I shrieked nonstop, along with the rest of my Beatle soul mates.

My god, how I *loved* those gals! (With their surprisingly long skirts—I thought everyone wore miniskirts back then—and their little rounded collars and their I LOVE THE BEATLES! buttons)

We were all in this together, and for the next incredible half hour (that's all the time the Beatles played for!), we jumped and yelled and reached out for the stage and hit each other and were in a totally blissed-out state.

At one point, a girl two rows in front of me gave in to the hysteria, crumpled like a rag doll, and disappeared below the bobbing heads and waving arms.

The girl behind me clutched my shoulders throughout the concert, probably to prevent herself from falling down in a Beatles-induced swoon.

I didn't faint myself, but by the end of the concert I had tears, *real tears*, in my eyes. How could I not? I had just heard the Beatles play "If I Fell" and "All My Loving" and "She Loves You" and about nine other songs. And man, were they good. Truly.

Those guys could play. In the prime of their early rock 'n' roll days—which is where they were when I saw them at the Bowl—they were an absolutely great live band.

The whole experience was beyond wild. It was like being on another planet. Actually, it was more like being in . . .

Heaven

28

As soon as that thought occurred to me—and it did, right in the middle of the Beatles' final song, "Twist and Shout"—it was gone. All of it.

The crowd.
The Beatles.
The music.

As quickly as it had appeared, it disappeared, and I found myself standing on my bleacher seat in the middle of an empty amphitheater. I looked around in shock. I felt like a little girl who'd been deserted after an especially wild and wonderful party.

Suddenly, I collapsed into a slumped sitting position on my wooden bleacher seat. I'd never screamed nonstop for half an hour before. It takes a lot out of you, let me tell you. I was drained. The muscles in my face hurt.

Spaced and numbed out, I sat in the middle of all that silence, going over and over in my head what I'd just seen and heard and felt.

"For my money, there has never been a better band."

I hadn't seen Abernathy approach. But there he was, as if appearing out of nowhere, standing in the wide aisle that separated my seating section from the one below and staring at the now-empty stage.

"Abernathy," I said in a surprised tone. He just stood there, his back to me. Then it hit me. What he said. "Did you just say, 'For my money, there has never been a better band'?"

It took Abernathy a while, but he finally turned, walked up to where I was sitting, and plopped down next to me.

"Yes, that's what I said."

I let his reply sink in, then asked, "So you're telling me you saw the Beatles just now?" Abernathy nodded. I studied Abernathy with a frown. He had the same shape. Same face. But he looked different somehow. Felt different. "What's going on here?" I finally asked. "Who *are* you, Abernathy?" I was kinda scared at that point, to be honest.

Abernathy didn't answer at first. But then, with a reassuring smile, he said, "I'm your Fairy Godmother, Regina. Well, obviously I'm your Fairy God*father*. But girls tend to prefer Fairy Godmothers, so that's usually what I e-mail them."

Can you believe that? I was totally blindsided by Abernathy's revelation.

"I didn't tell you earlier because you needed to take this journey on your own. Figure things out on your own. Otherwise, none of this would have any meaning."

I very quickly accepted that Abernathy was telling me the truth. And why not? Why would he lie about something like that? Besides, Abernathy now had this vibe about him. It felt . . . otherworldly, sitting next to him.

So we just sat, silent, for a bit. The wind had stopped blowing through the trees and it was just so, so quiet. I was running a lot of things through my head. Things I wanted to ask Abernathy. I think Abernathy wanted me to ask those things, whatever they were. That's the impression I got from him as he sat, silent as a Buddha, the warmth from his body reaching out and enveloping me, like an embrace.

Then something occurred to me. It was like playing Rubik's Cube, that kind of game, when all of a sudden, when you least expect it, *bam*. There you are, staring at six solid colors. This thought of mine was like that. *Bam*. All of a sudden. A six-solid-color revelation.

"Wait a second, Abernathy." He looked at me, slow and easy. "I know why you brought me here tonight." Abernathy didn't say a word. Just looked at me. "You want me to go back to Twin Oaks. You wanted me to see the Beatles, see how great they were."

"This journey isn't about what I want, Regina. It's about what you want. Rory from the Instigators is still here, isn't he? And Trey? On the other hand, the new Bono decided to go home. They made up their own minds. I didn't tell them what to do, one way or the other. As for tonight, I just wanted to treat you to a very special concert the night before you decide what *you're* going to do."

"I already know what I'm going to do."

"Do you?"

I knew I was in for it when Abernathy said that. I looked into his warm, wise, loving eyes and could tell that Abernathy . . . was all knowing. I could just feel that. And if that were the case, he knew everything I'd been thinking about and going through on my journey and he knew I had recently had some doubts about my decision to accept those Grammys and stay in L.A. They were just little hints of doubts, but they were there.

And I didn't want them to be there!

So I said firmly, stubbornly, "Yes, Abernathy. I know what I'm going to do."

"OK." Abernathy smiled and nodded. End of discussion. He stood up and started down the steps. He was almost to the bottom of the aisle when I called out, "Abernathy?" He turned slowly and looked up at me. "Let's just say, hypothetically speaking, that I did decide to go back. Which I'm not! What do I do? Send you an e-mail?"

Abernathy took a little time before he shook his head no.

"It's a little more complicated than that."

"So what, then?"

"You have to figure that out yourself."

"What? You've gotta be kidding me."

"Remember, Regina, one of the things your wish come true can be is a game. You don't help someone finish a game, do you? They have to finish it themselves." I must have looked a bit annoyed at his answer, because Abernathy followed that up with "I'll give you a hint." Like a seasoned entertainer, Abernathy paused for just the right amount of time, then said, "Believe in yourself."

You might think I was disappointed hearing Abernathy

feed me such a cliché. *Believe in yourself.* How many times have you heard that? But coming from Abernathy, it was as though I heard it for the first time. There was a primal power to it.

Believe . . .
in . . .
yourself.

I frowned, thinking about those three words. Why did Abernathy tell me that? What kind of hint was it? Suddenly, the air seemed to go out of the amphitheater. It was a similar sensation to the one that preceded my jump to the Beatles concert, actually. And just like that . . .

Abernathy was gone. I studied the immediate area with a frown. I looked all around the Bowl. No Abernathy in sight. I stood up, went down the steps, and walked along the gently curving aisle and exited the Bowl the same way I had come in.

Still no sign of my Fairy Godfather. But I had seen the limo from my higher-up ramp's vantage point. That made me feel better. I didn't think Abernathy would just leave like that.

But when I got to the Hummer, Abernathy wasn't in the driver's seat. I opened the back door and peered into the dark interior. No one there. I looked around at the empty parking lot, suddenly feeling like I was the lone figure in the center of a still-life landscape.

The wind had started up again. The trees were once again singing their mysterious, whispering song. The moon was lower in the sky, and it had gotten very cold. I shivered and got into the Hummer to warm myself up. Fortunately, the keys were in the ignition. I turned on the engine and studied the dash to find the HEAT button.

There was a screen in the center of the dash for a GPS system. I was looking for the heater when the screen suddenly turned itself on. Instead of a map to some unknown destination, however, there was a message. It read:

Sorry, Regina, but I had to go. An emergency in the superhero wish world. I know you'll do the right thing. Love, Abernathy

Superhero wish world? What a wacky universe Abernathy was in charge of! That kind of responsibility would make a person plenty busy, but still . . . Abernathy had left me. What did he expect, I should drive myself back to the hotel? All I had was a Cinderella license!

Believe in yourself.

I'm pretty sure Abernathy sent me that thought. It felt like it, anyway, like the time he helped me over the hump at the T.J. concert.

OK. Right. Believe in myself. Got it. This was a little test, that's all. Another part of Abernathy's game. This could be fun. Driving a mile-long Hummer through the streets of L.A. at five thirty in the morning. *I can do this.* I sat and stared at all of the dials and gadgets in front of me. It was like being in the cockpit of an airplane.

One step at a time. That's how you get somewhere. At least that's what I told myself as I tried to figure out what to do to get my white behemoth going. I'd already turned on the ignition. Now I put the gear in reverse and released the brake.

Oh, boy, here we go.

29

Luckily, it was early in the morning. I didn't have a ton of traffic to deal with. But before even getting to the streets, it took me forever to turn the Hummer around in the huge, empty parking lot. I felt like Austin Powers trying to turn that electric car around in the hallway. Bigger vehicle. Same concept.

When I finally got the metal monstrosity pointed in the right direction, I drove slowly out of the deserted lot. (Strangely, the security guard was absent from his post.)

OK. So far, so good. But then, when I turned from the driveway onto Highland Avenue . . .

SCREEEEEEEEECH!!!

That was the Hummer trading paint with a traffic-light pole. I almost lost control of the wheel at that point.

It's OK, Regina. Just a little sideswiping moment. Everything's cool. You can do this!

I managed to steady her out and continued down Highland,

even though I was in hyper-breathing mode. Fortunately, Highland's a pretty straight street, so I didn't have any further traffic violation incidents. At least, until I had to turn onto Sunset.

CRAAAAAASSH!!!

Trash can! The kind that's bolted to the sidewalk. My heart jumped into my throat when that happened. *My god*, I thought. *What if the police stop me? How will I explain this to them? Wait, what's that sound? That* screeching *sound?*

I was leaning over the steering wheel at that point, my entire body in spasm, my hands clutching the wheel so hard that my knuckles had turned white.

Ohmygod. The trash can's caught under the car!

And it was. The ripped-from-its-foundation can was being dragged under the limo's frame.

SCREEEEEEEEEEEEECCH!!!

I was so mortified that I wished a hole would open up right there on Sunset and swallow me and the limo whole. I didn't think that would happen, so I drove slow as a snail down beginning-to-get-busy Sunset as the metal trash can continued its nails-against-a-blackboard screeching on the asphalt street. An atonal symphony that drew quizzical, annoyed stares from the few people who were out at this hour.

When the Sheraton finally came into view, I laughed out loud. Maybe it was all the tension and stress being released.

Maybe the absurdity of driving a Hummer limo down Sunset Boulevard at six in the morning finally revealed itself to me. Whichever, that one short laugh built steadily into a laughing jag by the time I got to the hotel.

I found it hilarious when I bounced jauntily over the curb after misjudging the entrance to the circular driveway. I thought it was hysterical when I parked in front of the entrance, staggered out from behind the driver's seat, and saw the twisted remains of the trash can wedged next to the rear tire.

The astonished concierge must have thought I was totally gone when I handed him the key to the Hummer, by then trading mirthful giggles with hacking coughs.

WHEW!

When the elevator doors opened on my floor, I wiped the back of my hand across my forehead in an exaggerated way that said, *Glad's that's over!* My evening out had left me feeling like a drunk.

The Beatles concert. (Incredible!)
Meeting my Fairy Godfather. (Surrrrr-prise!)
The drive home. (Slapstick time!)

I walked on unsteady legs down the hall to my room. It took me several tries to get the card into the slot to open the door. I was so out of it, I was cross-eyed.

When I finally got into my room, all I wanted to do was fall onto my bed and conk out. But I didn't. A thin shaft of light was blazing on the curtain that covered the balcony door. In the time that it had taken me to go into the hotel, come up the elevator, and get to my room, sunrise had happened.

I opened the curtain. Dust particles danced in the laserlike beam of light that burst happily into the room. I slid open the door and went out onto the balcony.

Wow.

It was beautiful. A brilliant, red half circle of sun was peeking over the distant eastern horizon. It smelled like sunrise. A fresh new scent was in the air. I smiled and leaned on the railing. Was this great or what?

This . . . was the beginning of a new day. The beginning of *the* day. The beginning of the first day of the rest of my life! (You get the idea.) I felt tired and goofy and glad to be alive. As I watched the sun gradually reveal itself in all its full-circle glory, it dawned on me that I'd just pulled an all-nighter (except for the little bit of time when I dreamed my Saturday Night at the Movies dream).

When was the last time I'd done that? Without much effort, my last dusk till dawn came to me. It was shortly after I had formed the Caverns. We had practiced all night down in my basement. We played electric until Dad told us to shut it down, then we went acoustic.

What a blast that had been. We were full of spunk and high promise and were gonna take on the world. And when the sun came up, Julian drove us to evil McDonald's, and we had egg McMuffins and coffee and all kinds of food that was bad for you. That was the night I fell in love with Julian.

Julian . . .

I thought about Julian for a while as I stood on the balcony, and the street below came more and more to life. I thought about Julian's song. His really, really good song. That stirred something in me. But I was way too tired to deal with another mysterious what-is-it? kind of feeling. (I'd had a lot of those lately.) Besides, one thing I discovered that morning standing on the Sheraton balcony is that sunrises quickly lose their happy-face, ain't-this-special, aren't-you-glad-to-be-alive feeling. And what's left in place of that feeling is exhaustion.

So I went back inside, took off my clothes, and collapsed into bed. As I snuggled under the covers, I began a lullaby-like mantra.

Which Grammy will I win first?
Which Grammy will I win first?

I figured the mantra would prevent any doubts from creeping in and spoiling my sleep or my decision to stay in L.A. to officially begin my great new famous life.

Still, like a kid who's had a riddle dangled in front of her, I couldn't help but wonder . . . what *did* Abernathy's parting hint mean?

Believe in yourself.
Which Grammy will I win first?
Believe in yourself.
Which Grammy will I win first?
Believe in yourself.

Those two sentences duked it out in my head, threatening to keep me up for some time. But they didn't. Before I knew it, I . . .

(*Asleep.*)

30

A circle of figures above me. Conspiratorial whispers. What felt like a dream wasn't. As I woke, the people around me slowly came into focus.

Trey and Mom and Dad. All with concerned expressions. I smiled at them and stretched slowly, *languorously*, I believe is the word. "Morning," I greeted them, my voice sounding thick and heavy, like it had come out in slow motion. I felt groggy, but good, like I had just woken from a sleep cure or something.

"It's not *morning*," Trey scolded. "It's two in the afternoon! You have to be at the Shrine in two hours!"

"And I will be," I assured him, totally unconcerned, then rolled over onto my stomach.

"Regina, what is wrong with you?" That was Mom.

"Nothing, Mother," I mumbled into the pillow. "Everything is absolutely first-rate."

"We have to get her up," Trey said sternly, up above me somewhere in the clouds. I felt myself being picked up and put on my feet. Dad balanced me on one side, Trey on the other.

"Really, Regina," Dad said softly. "How do you feel?"

"Really good, Dad. I do. Don't worry 'bout a thing. Just leave me be, and I'll get ready for my big day. Or night, rather."

Everyone looked pretty skeptical about my ability to get myself ready. It didn't help matters when I gave them all a big, goofy grin and fell back onto the bed.

"That does it!" Trey said in disgust. "I'm calling a doctor."

"Unnecessary," I insisted. "I will be ready as rain in two hours to go to the Shrine Auditorium." Then I began to sing, *"If the rain comes, they run and hide their heads . . ."*

"She must have taken something," Trey whispered to Dad.

"I'm right here, Trey," I called out to him. "I can hear you. And, no, I didn't take anything. Now *go*. Please!"

Trey stared down at me for a moment. "Stay with her, Laura," he commanded my mother. "If she's still acting like this in fifteen minutes, call me."

"You should salute Master Trey, Mom. What he says, goes. After all, he gets all the new acts that come to town. Don't you, Trey?"

I'm not sure why I said that. Maybe because Trey was getting on my nerves. But in that instant, Trey knew that I knew. His eyes narrowed like a cat's, and he drilled me with a glare. "Don't forget, Regina. This *is* a big day for you."

"I know. Don't you worry your little pocketbook about that." There was a tense face-off between me and Trey, then he pointed to a clothes bag that hung over a nearby chair. "I brought you some decent clothes to wear to the Grammys. Pick something out. It's time to stop wearing T-shirts and tutus and little-girl clothes. You're a young woman now. Start dressing like it." Trey spun around and walked out of the room.

"I do not like that guy," Dad said.

"Well, I do," Mom countered. "Why were you baiting him like that, Regina?"

"He was getting on my nerves. Besides, I wanted to spend a little quality time with my mom and dad."

My comment made Mom shift uncomfortably and ease slightly away from Dad. Which did not go unnoticed by my father. "I need to go see how Julian and Danny are doing," Dad said. "See you soon."

After Dad left, Mom crossed her arms and looked at me with a frown. "What's going on with you? You're acting very strange."

It was a valid question. Why was I acting all goofy and drunk-like and saying exactly what was on my mind? That wasn't at all like me. "I don't know," I replied. "Maybe if I wasn't acting like this, I'd totally collapse in hysteria and nervousness."

That answer seemed to appease Mom. As it turned out, it was right on the mark, which I would soon discover. I sat up in bed, suddenly serious, and started to trace a figure eight pattern on the bedcover. "By the way, Mom. Dad and I had a nice talk yesterday."

"What about?" Mom immediately tensed in a defensive pose.

"He said he wasn't going to try to stop me from buying a house here and living with you."

"Why did he say that?" Mom's reply was sharp and suspicious.

" 'Cause he thinks I'll be happier here. And he said he wants to make peace with you. So he'll be welcome when he comes to visit." Mom was silent. "I want you to be nice to him, Mom. I want things to change."

Mom visibly bristled. "Just because you're big stuff now doesn't mean you can order me around."

"It's not an order. It's a necessary request. I mean, why does it have to be like this? Why do you and Dad act like you're enemies or something? It feels so terrible."

Anything you want it to be . . .

At that moment in my journey, I wanted it to be about reconciliation. Between Mom and Dad. Without warning, I started to cry. It surprised me, that bubbling up of emotion from somewhere deep inside me, from that mysterious place where feelings reside. Mom immediately shed her defensive and suspicious posturing. She sat next to me on the bed and held me.

"This isn't just about me and you, Mom," I managed to get out between my sniffling and quick intakes of breath. "It isn't just about us getting together after all these years and acting like two sisters or something. Dad's part of this, too, you know. Whether you like it or not."

"It's OK," Mom said, rocking me slightly as she held me around the shoulders. "It's gonna be OK."

I actually believed her. Not in a happily-ever-after kind of way, like Mom and Dad getting back together and remarrying or anything like that. I had hoped and prayed for that for quite a while after they had separated, but at some point, it dawned on me that wasn't going to happen. But as I sat with

Mom on the bed, in her arms, I did feel like things could change between her and Dad. That they could be more like friends. And that I had the power to make things change.

That was it!

That was the answer, I realized with a jolt. All these years I'd been waiting for Dad or Mom to make the move. To start behaving more civil, more friendly, toward each other. They were the adults, after all. But suddenly, I knew it was *me*. I had to make the move. For all of us.

I had the power.

Ironic that I had that revelation the same moment I was blubbering like a baby. But after my little breakdown, I felt calmer and kind of cleaned out and satisfied, sort of like how it feels after one of those summer storms blow in suddenly, rattle the windows, then is gone before you know it.

Predictably, Mom looked self-conscious holding me after I stopped crying and had blown my nose loudly right next to her ear. She really is not the most affectionate person in the world. But I can't hold that against her. She gave me a little smile and slid off the bed.

"Well," she said, smoothing out her too-short-for-her-age skirt. "You be OK? Can I go get ready for the big night?"

"Of course."

"Trey said you were supposed to have your hair done at one. It's past two, so *that* ain't gonna happen. Need any help?"

"No, that's OK."

"Sure?"

"Positive, Mom."

Mom gave me a wave as she headed for the door. "I'll see you at the Grammys, then."

"Why don't you ride with us in the limo?" I asked.

Mom thought about that, then said, "OK. I think I will."

"Good."

"Good." Mom smiled, then was gone.

I sighed and looked around the room after Mom left. Everything was the same but looked different somehow. I guess because *I* felt different. Not a hundred percent different. Not even fifty percent. Just a little different. Sometimes that's all you need, I guess.

I looked at the digital clock by the bed. In less than three hours, I would be on the stage at the Shrine Auditorium. My journey, my wish come true, was almost at its end.

Its end.

Yes, it was time for me to go back to Twin Oaks.

I didn't realize that in a big, thunderclap, aha kind of moment. It was a quiet and simple moment and just like that, it was crystal clear to me that I'd only been pretending that I was staying.

Don't get me wrong. I had totally convinced myself that I was going to start a new life in L.A. with Mom and Bradley and all my new, best friends. But that had only been a pose. Abernathy, wise man that he was, knew that before I did.

Still, he had left me alone to figure out the last piece of the puzzle by myself. The last move I had to make to finish my rock 'n' roll game and reach my final destination.

Home.

31

Like most people, I've made some New Year's resolutions over the years. Last year I decided I was going to train to run a marathon. The year before, I was going to go out for the school play. *Every* year I convince myself that this is the year I'm going to play some of my songs to someone other than myself.

It takes energy to sustain charades like that. That's what they all turned out to be, I'm sorry to say, the above resolutions. I never wound up doing them. But the thing is, once I had let those resolutions go and concentrated on the things that I decided were actually doable, it was like a weight had been lifted from my shoulders.

That's how I felt after I knew my wish come true was coming to an end. My charade of thinking I was staying was gone and I felt kind of free, in a way. But there was still stuff to do, like try to figure out *how* I was gonna get back home.

Before that, however, I needed to get ready for the Grammys. After a quick, aghast look through the clothes Trey had brought, I knew I'd be wearing something I brought from home. (The skirts and tops looked like something from *P.C.H.*)

It was after I had my outfit selected and was laying it out on my bed that I saw Stuart's CD on the floor. It was barely visible under the side bed table. I felt guilty when I saw the CD. I'd never listened to the songs. Never called Stuart.

I picked up the CD, put it in my laptop, and took the laptop into the bathroom so I could listen to Stuart's songs while I worked on my hair. Even though Stuart lived in this wacky world of make-believe, *he* didn't know that, right? Maybe it would mean something to him to get a few words of encouragement.

I had my hands over my head, brushing out my hair, when the first song came on. I froze at the sound of the guitar strumming the opening chords to a song called "No Drama." I knew the name of the song *because I had written it.* Totally stunned, I stood in front of the mirror and listened to Stuart play and sing my song.

How on earth did he know it? I'd never played it for anyone. After listening for a few minutes, I got over the shock of hearing someone other than myself play one of my songs. The more I listened to "No Drama," the more I thought, *Sounds pretty good, actually.* Of all my songs, I think it's maybe my best.

The next song was another one of mine. And the next. I was so caught up in listening to Stuart's interpretations of my songs that I literally jumped when someone pounded on my door.

It was Dad. He was shocked to see me open my door in my underwear, with half my hair brushed and the other half exploding from my head like a fright wig.

"Regina. We're leaving in half an hour!"

"I'll be ready. Look. There's my clothes, all laid out." I pointed to them proudly. Dad looked skeptically at my costume choice, which was basically a pair of jeans and a ratty T-shirt. "Don't worry. I'll be down in the lobby in half an hour." I gave Dad a smile and shut the door on him.

My false smile immediately faded. A jumble of emotions and questions were fighting it out in my head. The most immediate question was . . .

How did *Stuart know my songs?*

I went back to the bathroom, took the CD out of the player, picked up the bathroom phone, and punched in Stuart's number, which he had written on the CD. I tapped my foot nervously as I waited for him to answer. Then I heard:

"Hello, Regina." It was a recording. Abernathy's voice. "This must mean that you listened to the CD. But before you were able to do that, you had to take the time to stop and talk to a young man who desperately wanted to get his music to you. Not everybody who has come here, to this world, has done that. The Instigators' Rory, for example. But you did. You have a good heart, Regina. You might have been seduced a bit by your L.A. trip, but you never really lost the essence of who you are. That essence is in your songs. Don't ever forget that. They're good because they're *you.*"

There was silence for a moment, then Abernathy said, "By the way, in case you haven't figured it out, I was Stuart." Another brief moment of silence. "Oh, and I was also the oboe player. But the girl the security guards almost stopped from getting to you? That was you. The original Regina." The tape clicked off, and I stood in the middle of the bathroom, holding the phone.

Nice, Abernathy, I thought. *Very, very clever.*

But also very, very confusing. What did it all mean? Maybe nothing. Maybe Stuart and the oboe player and the original Regina were just random "moves" in my wish-come-true fantasy game. But then, in another six-solid-color moment, it came to me. Stuart's—or, rather, Abernathy's—CD was not a random thing. It was a clue. A clue to what I had to do to get back to Twin Oaks.

I suddenly felt weak in the knees. If I was right about this, Abernathy was not making my last day in La-la Land an easy one. If I was right, maybe this was the price I had to pay for taking such an incredible journey. If I was right, I hoped one thing.

That I was up to it.

32

My heel tapped nervously. My knee went updownupdownup-
downupdown. I sat in the back of the limo between Julian
and Danny. Mom and Dad were across from us. Not sitting
too close, but they were together, anyway, in the same place at
the same time and not arguing, so that was good. I hoped that
I was looking at the future. That when I got back to Twin
Oaks, *if* I got back, this is what I would eventually see. Mom
and Dad, sometimes in the same place at the same time, sort
of friendly to each other. I knew now that it was up to me to
see that that happened.

Anyway, we had a new driver. That wasn't a surprise. I had
a feeling I wouldn't be seeing Abernathy anymore. Which
made me feel pretty lonely. And very, very nervous. Actually,
I was beyond nervous. I couldn't believe what I had to do once
I got to the Shrine. Or at least what I thought I had to do. And,
seeing as I couldn't confide in anyone, that made me feel even
worse. It does help to unload all your problems on someone
when you're feeling bad or uptight or out of sorts. But this . . .
this I had to bear all by myself.

Maybe that was the idea.

"Slightly out of control." "Partylike atmosphere." "Disorienting, but exciting." Those were some of the phrases I used to describe the vibes at the Shrine the day before during our rehearsal. I suppose I could use those same words to describe the Shrine the night of the Grammys.

Times *one hundred*, maybe!

You've seen the Grammys on TV, right? Maybe you've checked out some of the red-carpet shows before the Grammys. If so, you have some idea what it's like. But let me tell you, nothing could have prepared me for the burst of energy and excitement and screaming fans and jostling paparazzi when we arrived at the Shrine.

The best way of describing what it was like would be to run it past you like a series of snapshots. That's what it felt like when we arrived at the Shrine Auditorium. The whole scene was so completely overwhelming that I wasn't able to process it in a normal kind of way. It wasn't like slow motion. Or fast motion. It was more like . . .

POP! (Pulling up to the Shrine.)

POP! (Getting out of the limo.)

POP! POP!! (Heading down the red carpet.)

POP! POP!! POP!!! (Photographers blinding us with flashbulbs.)

POP! POP!! (Microphones being shoved into our faces by one celebrity interviewer after another.)

POP! POP!! POP!!! (Fans screaming!)

POP! (Suddenly inside the crowded Shrine lobby.)
POP! (A young guy in a uniform leading us through the crush of people.)
POP! POP!! (Finally. Backstage. Cocoonlike darkness.)
WHEW!

That's when things returned to their normal rhythm, relatively speaking, and I was able to breathe a bit. But my little oasis of calm didn't last very long. That's because Trey appeared out of the darkness and asked to have a word with me. It wasn't a pleasant word, either. And believe me, it would test my resolve to do what I had come to the Shrine to do.

33

"What was that all about back at the hotel!" Trey hissed in my ear after pulling me around a curtain at the side of the Shrine stage. The look on his face was really scary. He looked like he wanted to hit me. "Just because you know about me doesn't mean you can get flip. Understand? I know about you, too. Remember that."

I realized that Trey still had a firm grip on my arm. I yanked it away from him.

"It was Rory, wasn't it?" Trey said disdainfully. "He's the one who told you."

"None of your business." I was starting to boil with a hatred for Trey.

"This is *all* my business! And don't you forget it!" Trey took a deep breath to calm himself. "Much as I'd love to continue our little chat, you obviously need to get ready for your opening number. In the future, my dear? It's customary to get dressed *before* you arrive at an event."

I wanted to wipe Trey's sarcastic expression right off his face. So I did.

"I don't need to get ready," I said. "I *am* ready."

Trey's mouth literally fell open when I said that. My jeans and old T-shirt—a pre-wish gift from Julian with *The Caverns* painted on it, just like the one Julian had worn the night we played T.J. back in Twin Oaks—was the polar opposite of glammed out. Plus, I was wearing hardly any makeup. But that's how I wanted to present myself to the millions of Grammy viewers.

Trey's shock morphed into a smile. "Ohhhhh, OK. I get it. Very good, Regina. You think you're going home, don't you?" Trey sounded like he was talking to a child. "Well, I have a news flash for you, honey. No way do you have it in you to do what you think you're going to do."

Trey's smile was actually scarier than his frown. Backlit by red stage lights, he truly looked like . . . well, I know it was my overactive imagination, but he looked like the devil to me in that moment. I felt small in his presence, that's for sure. His powerful persona seemed to drain the energy and confidence from me.

"I'm going out onstage looking just like I am," I insisted. But I could feel myself weakening every second I was with Trey.

"One bit of advice," Trey said calmly, confidently. "If I were you, I'd send for those little outfits I got you. Then I'd get my butt to hair and makeup. Then I'd thank my lucky stars I was given this opportunity. Because without all of this, Regina?" Trey leaned toward me until his mouth was practically kissing my ear, then he whispered, "You're just ordinary."

I felt like I'd been hit in the stomach by a heavyweight. My legs went all rubbery and I got light-headed and I really thought I'd have to sit down right there on the hardwood floor of the Shrine stage. Trey gave me a final hard glare, then turned and walked away. As I watched him stop to say hello to Eminem, I totally panicked. I hated myself for my weakness, but I knew Trey had broken me over his knee like a stick.

What were you thinking, Regina? You can't do this! You don't have the guts, the confidence, to do this! Trey's right!

I actually took a few steps toward Trey at that moment. I was going to grab him and tell him I was just joking. Of course, I was going to mask my imperfections and try to look as perfect as possible. Of course, I was thanking my lucky stars for this opportunity.

But then . . . I stopped.

Stand your ground, Regina. I urged myself. I wasn't really sure if I could, though. Standing in the darkness of the backstage area, looking at all of the beautiful, famous people, I experienced a final, crook-of-the-finger, come-join-us moment. It was all just a Grammy away.

How I managed to resist that last come-on, I don't know. But I did. I didn't go throw myself at Trey's feet. I didn't make peace with him. Believe me, it was one of the hardest things I ever did. Scratch that. It *was* the hardest thing I ever did.

I leaned up against the back wall of the Shrine stage and closed my eyes. I still felt weak and shaky and now kind of exhausted, like I'd just been through a battle of some sort. OK, so maybe I had managed to resist Trey, but did I have the energy to go the rest of the way? To do what I needed to do to finish this thing?

As I stood there feeling invisible in the midst of all the swirling activity and the multicolored overhead lights, I heard:

Believe . . .
in . . .
yourself.

I didn't just think I heard that, either. Coming from out of nowhere, I literally heard Abernathy's voice. It was like Luke hearing Obi-Wan say, "Believe in the Force!" I couldn't help but smile. Abernathy was still with me! I wasn't alone, after all.

OK, Abernathy, I thought in reply. *I'll try. I'll try to go out onstage just as I am. And sing from my heart.*

But I wouldn't be singing "Hello, Goodbye." "No Drama" was going to be the Caverns' opening song. (Did you guess that?) *That's* what Stuart's (Abernathy's) CD had told me. That I needed to go out onstage, look millions of people right in the eye, and say, "Here I am, in all my ordinary glory. Take me . . . or leave me." Do you know how hard that is?

Of course you do.

Everyone does, from time to time.

34

"Regina?"

I was pacing alongside the Caverns' dressing-room trailer that was parked in the back of the Shrine along with dozens of other trailers for "spillover" bands, artists, makeup, and TV people. Julian had come from around the corner of the trailer behind me. I stopped my pacing when I heard him say my name.

"You OK?" he asked after I turned to him. I nodded, but that was a lie. I felt like I would throw up, actually. And I wasn't fooling Julian, that's for sure. He walked over to me, put one hand on each of my shoulders, and said, "If it's any help, I'm really nervous, too."

Julian looked and smelled really good. I felt like hugging him. Instead I said, "Julian?"

"What?"

"Nothing. Forget it. Never mind."

"You can't do that, Regina."

Actually, I couldn't believe what I was thinking at that particular moment, but I was, so I asked, "Are you in love with Hayley?" It was a question I had wanted to ask ever since I knew there *was* a Hayley.

Julian sighed. He smiled, in a sad kind of way, and said, "You know I'm not."

"No, I don't, Julian. I wouldn't have asked you if I did."

Julian gave me a soulful, deep-in-the-eyes kind of look. After what seemed like a very long time, he said, very softly, "Don't you know, Regina? I've never gotten over you."

It was one of those incredible, this-doesn't-happen-but-maybe-a-few-times-in-a-lifetime moments. A moment when you hear someone say exactly what you want to hear them say. I wanted to kiss Julian. *Needed* to kiss him. If not now . . . when? When would there be a better time?

But I held back. Just like I had all those other times when I felt like kissing Julian. Back in my old Twin Oaks life. I knew the moment, the fleeting moment, would be gone before I could blink.

You have the power, Regina.

And just like that, I did it. I kissed Julian.

I caught him by surprise, I could tell, and he instinctively pulled back a bit. But I held on tight, like my life depended on it, which in some ways it did at that moment. Maybe Julian realized there was no way I was letting go. Maybe he could feel that I was for real. That I really meant this kiss. All I know is, after a moment . . . he returned it. That completed the kiss. Made it whole. It became a *real* kiss then.

It wasn't like my kiss with Bradley on the pier, or at Bradley's house. It wasn't as intense, as explosive, as assured as those. But it was definitely better than the ones with Bradley.

It was more tender. But, ironically, it seemed to have more *weight*. In short, it was everything I had imagined it would be. And more. When we parted, we looked at each other. A slow smile spread across our faces. But then . . .

I saw Bradley standing between two trailers about ten yards behind Julian! Shocked at what he had just seen, Bradley turned away and walked out of sight behind one of the trailers.

"Be right back!" I told Julian. I caught up with Bradley as he strode briskly toward a nearby parking lot full of cars and limos. "Bradley!"

He didn't respond.

"Bradley! Please!"

Bradley stopped, turned, and stared at me. I stopped a few feet from him. It might as well have been a hundred. We were both silent as technicians ran back and forth between the trailers with last-second preparations for the big show. Way in the background, someone yelled, "Caverns! You're on! *Now!*"

"Better go," Bradley said coldly.

"It just happened," I said.

"Yeah. Most things do."

We were silent for a moment, then Bradley said, "I can't believe you still like that guy."

"That guy has a name, you know."

"Yeah, I just can't remember what it is."

Bradley was being intentionally nasty at that point, which made me angry, but I held my anger in check. I didn't want to end all this with an argument.

"You know what, Bradley? I'll admit, I totally fell under

your spell. But you know it wouldn't have worked out between the two of us. We're both so completely different."

Bradley didn't say anything, which I took to mean he agreed with me. Which was OK. I knew that Bradley didn't love me—like he claimed he did that night on the phone message—he just loved the idea of having a famous rock star for a girlfriend. And to be honest? I kind of liked the idea of having a famous actor for a boyfriend. At least, for a little while.

"*Caverns*!!!" yelled the frantic production assistant, or whoever it was trying to track us down. "*Get your asses in here*!!!!"

"So . . . ," I said. "Guess I'll be seeing you."

"Yes, you will. Every Thursday night on the number-one-rated show in its time slot."

With that, Bradley gave me one of his killer smiles. I watched him walk away, toward the rear entrance of the Shrine. There was a huge group of fans and paparazzi on a nearby sidewalk, kept out of the compound by a metal fence. When they yelled out to Bradley, he strolled over to them and started signing pieces of paper and whatever else they shoved in his face. I shook my head and smiled at the sight. Bradley was right where he wanted to be. Feeling all the heat from his fans. As long as he had that, it meant he was famous.

"Regina!" I turned to see Julian gesturing animatedly from a few trailers away. "Gotta go!"

As I ran with Julian toward the Shrine, I felt loose and free and energized, like I could run all the way back to Twin Oaks, just as long as Julian didn't leave my side. But there was something I obviously needed to do before returning to Twin Oaks.

"I have a surprise for you, Julian." He gave me a look that asked, *Now what?* "Don't freak out or anything, but there's been a little change in the program."

35

I stood on a pitch-black stage. The void in front of me was filled with the excited buzz of a massive amount of people. In just a few seconds, they would be illuminated by an explosion of light and color. Before that, however, I would be throwing a major monkey wrench into the grand opening of a program that was being beamed into millions of households.

But I was ready. As ready as I'd ever be.

"Ladies and gentlemen . . . fellow musicians . . . fans from around the world . . . welcome to the Grammy Awards!"

The voice—floating, coming from nowhere—boomed out into the darkness. This was the moment when I was supposed to yell out, "One, two, three, four!" and start singing "Hello, Goodbye." Get it? "Hello?" At the beginning of the Grammy show?

But instead I slashed my electric guitar with the musical intro to "No Drama." I had told Julian and Waverly the chords to the song and instructed Danny that we were playing a rock song instead of "Hello, Goodbye" and to just do whatever he felt like. No coaching or lording over his creativity on this song. No, sir!

The stage and auditorium were still cloaked in darkness as the band fell in tentatively behind me and started to fill in the spaces suggested by my intro. It felt really ragged, that's for sure. And I felt a brief flash of panic. What if the first original song I ever played in public was a total stinker?

Don't think, Regina! Just play!

Right, right. Exactly. The captain of the ship. As I stepped up to the mic to start singing the first verse of the song, I could hear a frantic rushing about in the wings of the stage. I could only imagine the surprised, confused looks on those headset people's faces. Well, I'd be seeing them soon enough. I suddenly yelled out, in time to the music, "One, two . . . one, two, three, four!" And then there were . . .

Lights!

Video screen!

Cheers and applause!

It felt good to hear the audience explode with a wave of applause, just like they were supposed to. But they weren't reacting to the song. I knew that. It was the brilliant theatrics of the moment. The blinding lights. The sight of the psychedelic images behind us. The loud, overpowering sound of guitars and drums, ragged as they were.

I knew things would settle down very quickly and then the audience would be concentrating on just the song. So it was time to put myself out there. Time to let the audience judge me. In other words, time to start singing.

So I did.

And you know what? Magic happened. Truly. Maybe it was Abernathy, helping me out like he did at T.J., but everything fell into place after I began singing the lyrics to "No Drama." It was like coming home.

I could feel my vocals surfacing from somewhere deep inside me. I could feel the band jell behind me, Waverly laying down a hard, solid foundation, Danny playing with a gleeful innocence (as though he'd just discovered there was something called drums), Julian improvising riffs to complement my straight-ahead rock 'n' roll rhythm guitar.

It . . . felt . . . so . . . good. *The song was actually working.*

And I realized, *this* is what it was all about. Everything I'd experienced in the past week, all the crazy things that had happened in my wish-come-true world . . . it was like all that stuff was in a funnel, swirling around and pointing to this very moment.

Enjoy the moment, Regina.

I did just that. The band played and I sang and I was so caught up in the moment that Abernathy—the true wizard behind all this—caught me by surprise. He saved the best for last, I'll hand him that. It happened when I turned to Julian and gestured for him to join me at my mic for the final chorus.

I couldn't believe what I was seeing. The psychedelic images from the video screen were bleeding out onto the stage! I stared in shock as the images swirled around behind Danny, then ventured farther out onto the stage, like multicolored fingers of mist.

Julian frowned at my astonished expression and followed my gaze around the stage. When he looked back at me, it was clear he didn't see what I saw. Whatever was happening, was happening to me only.

OK. Got it. From the looks of things, I was being sent home on a magic carpet ride! *Nice touch, Abernathy. Weird, but nice.*

I still needed to concentrate on the song, however. It helped that Julian was standing right next to me. As he and I sang the chorus, two psychedelic fingers of mist pulsated out from opposite sides of the stage, curved around the edges of the auditorium, and joined high up in the top balcony.

I was surprisingly calm, considering that in addition to the psychedelic takeover of the top, and now the lower, balcony, the edges of my vision had started to bleed like a watercolor. It didn't feel like I had to hurry the song to its conclusion. Matter of fact, I sensed that I had a bit more time before . . . what? Was I just gonna be whisked away in all this twisting, undulating miasma of color? A musical equivalent of Dorothy returning to Kansas?

I wasn't sure, but as "No Drama" neared its end, I had a lightning flash of what I wanted to do with whatever time I had remaining in La-la Land. I slashed my guitar in a downward motion to bring the song to a thunderous conclusion. The audience applauded, and it didn't feel like polite applause, either. That felt good, of course, but I had other things on my mind than whether or not the crowd really liked "No Drama."

Things like jumping right in and starting another song before the Instigators began "Boulevard of Broken Dreams," which is what was supposed to happen at that point in the program. As the lights shifted to Rory and his group, I blasted out the opening guitar riff to Julian's song.

Julian was shocked, of course. So was Rory and the Insti-gators and all the headset people on the side of the stage. I saw one of them throw his hands up in the air in a way that said, *The girl's totally gone off!*

I ignored all of the side-stage glares and shaking heads, ran back to Waverly, yelled out the progression of chords to him, then urged Danny to join in. Danny's a gamer, I'll say that. He's always up for anything. So he jumped right into it and started pounding the drums like he had a bone to pick with them or something.

I gestured to Julian to start singing his song. We'd hijacked the Grammys, and it was time to take it the rest of the way. Julian gave me a you're-actin'-kinda-crazy-here-Regina-but-I-think-I-like-it! look, then he stepped up to the mic.

I stood back and enjoyed what I figured would be the final moments in my wish-come-true world. By now the main floor of the auditorium was being taken over by the psychedelic mist. As for the balconies, they looked like they were being sucked around me and into the video screen!

I tried to ignore that rather strange sensation as I looked around and found Dad, standing at the side of the stage among the frantic headset people, who slashed their hands across their throats in a desperate attempt to get us to stop playing. Dad was obviously perplexed by my shenanigans, but he seemed more pleased and amused by them than any-thing.

Opposite Dad, in the other wing of the stage, was Trey. He shook his head in disgust when I looked at him. I gave him a big smile, which was not returned. Instead, he pointedly showed his back to me and walked off into the darkness. Which was where he belonged, as far as I was concerned.

Then there was Rory. I could be wrong, but I think I caught a hint of regret in his eyes when I glanced over and gave him a little wave. Not because I wasn't staying, but because he had made the choice to do just that.

Finally . . . Mom. She was sitting in the second row. She smiled and gave me an energetic thumbs-up, even though she looked confused about all the pandemonium she could see in the wings of the stage.

I started to tear up when I saw her. I looked down at my guitar. I didn't want Mom to see me cry. Besides, it was getting harder to focus on the song at that point—things were really whipping into a frenzy in the auditorium—so I needed to be sure my fingers were going where they were supposed to.

It's OK, I told myself. *It's all OK. Just enjoy the ride.*

It was then that I heard Julian calling to me. I looked up and saw him gesturing. He wanted me to sing with him. I walked over and stood so close to him that we were touching. It was a good place to be in those final moments.

The lively mist had almost reached the stage. Practically everyone in the auditorium was gone, replaced by a hazy sort of nothingness. It was just the people in the first few rows, and now they were going, dissolving and pooling together. The way all of this looked reminded me of the kaleidoscope I had when I was a kid, with its endlessly shifting colors and patterns, which I loved to watch—twisting the end back and forth, back and forth—until it made me dizzy.

Actually, I was getting a little dizzy watching all this. But that was all right, because clearly the concert was over. There was nobody left to hear it! It was just me and Julian, the last ones to go. So I closed my eyes and had the absolutely warm, wonderful sensation of him and me joining together, like we were one.

What a feeling!

But it didn't last. Next thing I knew I was traveling. Very fast. But even though I had the sensation of blasting though time and space, I felt very peaceful, very still, somehow. So I gave into that feeling and let myself be taken wherever it was I was going.

Before long, everything around me began to get very bright. It was like I was being treated to the most dazzling sunrise imaginable. It was like I was heading right toward the *origin* of the sunrise.

Bright . . . brighter . . . brightest!!!

And then . . .

PART THREE

Home

"Should I tell him you'll call later?"

I slowly opened my eyes and saw Dad staring down at me. Looking at him, I was aware of a haziness around the perimeter of my vision. My mouth felt really dry, so dry that my tongue was stuck to the roof of my mouth. I gradually took stock of my surroundings.

I was in bed.

In my Twin Oaks bedroom.

Light was peeking around the edges of the curtains.

"Regina? You OK?"

Was I? Was I home? Truly and for real?

"Just a second, Dad." My voice sounded small and tinny. I rolled out of bed, went to the window, and opened the curtains. The light outside announced that it was morning. There'd been a heavy snowfall overnight. Julian's Falcon was parked by the curb. "Julian's here?" I asked.

"That's what I just told you. Are you feeling OK?"

I looked around the room. All things Caverns had been replaced with all things Beatles. If I had any doubt about whether or not I was back, truly back, that erased it.

"Yeah," I said. "I feel just fine."

Dad looked relieved. "Good. I was worried about you last night. I don't like seeing you down like that."

Last night? What happened last night? I glanced at my wall calendar and saw that it was December 22.

Okaaaaay, I thought. *Not only am I back, but it looks like I've returned to the morning after I made my wish!*

"Don't worry, Dad. I'm feeling much better now." And I was. I was feeling more and more normal as each minute passed. My vision was becoming clearer, sounds were returning to normal. But I was still really thirsty!

Dad smiled. "So what should I tell Julian? Want to call him later, after you've showered and had some breakfast?"

"No!"

Dad did a double take at my outburst. I smiled meekly and said, "I'll be down in two minutes." He nodded, a bit warily, then headed for the door. "Dad?" He turned and looked at me. I was going to tell him that I wanted to call Mom on Christmas and all three of us would get on the line together. But as we looked at each other, it didn't feel like the right time to bring that up. But that's what we would do, I knew. I wasn't expecting miracles. Just a new beginning.

So instead I told him, "I might need three minutes. Maybe four." Dad considered that, then said he would relay that information to Julian. After he left the room, I allowed myself to take a deep breath and appreciate the feeling of *being back.* I took a slow tour around my room, touching all of my Beatles posters and pictures, just to be sure they were real. I ended my tour at the shelf. The sight of all my Beatles stuff, the lunch boxes and miniature album covers with the bubble gum inside and, of course, my Beatle dolls, brought a smile to my face. I picked up my John Beatle doll and gave him a big kiss on his plastic face.

And that's when I saw it.

Back in the shadows, hidden behind the row of Beatle dolls, was another doll. Somehow I knew what it was before I even reached for it.

It was my Regina Bloomsbury Beatle doll. A note was taped to it. I opened the note and read,

Just a little memento from your trip. Congratulations, Regina. You made all the right moves.
Love, Abernathy

I stood for a while and stared at the note. Then I placed the Regina doll back where I had found it. A compound of emotions enveloped me. Relief and happiness and a hint of sadness and practically every emotion I had felt on my journey, all wrapped up in one wave, so suddenly overwhelming that I fell back on my bed, arms outspread as if I were falling off a stage onto a sea of waiting hands.

Then I saw, up above me on my ceiling, the *Magical Mystery Tour*–like rainbow I had painted when I was twelve or thirteen. *Perfect*, I thought with a smile. "Home" had been my Magical Mystery Tour all along.

A home that currently contained one Julian Armstrong, waiting for me downstairs! Mentally snapping back to the here and now, I grabbed my bright red sweatshirt and faded blue jeans from my now-depleted post-wish closet and dressed quickly.

Going down the stairs, I saw Julian standing in the middle of the living room, hands in his pockets, looking ill at ease. He had that just-got-up look. He looked irresistible. I had to remind myself, *He doesn't know anything that went on in L.A.*

"Hi," I said when I got to the living room.

Julian nodded hello.

"Want some coffee?"

Julian nodded again.

So I made a pot of coffee, and while I waited for it to brew, I drank a gallon of water to quench my strange post-wish thirst, and then Julian and I went down to the basement. It was really cold down there, but it felt wonderful just the same, being back in the heart and soul of the house.

Julian sat on the old sofa I had seen in my dream—the one I was sitting on with Mom and Dad watching *Help!* before they disappeared—his hands wrapped around the hot coffee mug for warmth. "So, anyway," he said, not looking at me. "I heard about your little scene with Lorna. Sorry it had to happen that way."

At first I thought Julian was talking about my catfight with Lorna in the limo. That wasn't it, of course. He was referring to my school hallway scene with Lorna, when she told me that she was quitting the Caverns. It felt like that had happened a very long time ago.

I sat next to Julian on the sofa. "So, what . . . you came over to see if I was OK?"

Julian looked at me then. Staring into Julian's blue-green eyes, I went all mushy and warm inside. (Cold? It wasn't cold in the Cavern!)

"Yeah," Julian finally said. "I guess I did."

I came to realize, in the days that followed, that my journey to L.A. was like a jewel. In the sense that when you turn a jewel very slowly, you are able see different facets, different colors, depending on the angle.

If I turned my journey one way, there was Mom and I. Turn it another, there was Dad and I. Another, me and my music. Turn it yet another . . .

Me and Julian.

One very important thing I learned on my wish-world trip was to not always wait for people to initiate things. Sometimes you have to take matters into your own hands. Or, in this case, arms.

There was a déjà vu–like feeling when I leaned over and kissed Julian. Just like our kiss behind the Shrine, I surprised Julian and he instinctively pulled back a bit. But I didn't retreat, and after a moment, everything fell into place, just like it had before. Julian returned the kiss. And it became whole.

Beauty.

It was as good as the Shrine kiss. No. Better. Because there, in the Cavern, *it was really happening.* When we finally parted, Julian looked kinda flushed. Actually, he looked kinda gorgeous is what he looked.

Smiles spread across our faces, and I thought, *OK, if that's all I got from my journey, the courage to give the boy of my dreams a kiss, it was well worth it.*

But I knew I'd gotten a lot more than that. When my inner electrical system calmed down a bit, I said, "Want to jam? Play some music?" It was like an offering. A celebration of the moment. But I couldn't read Julian's expression. I couldn't tell if he wanted to play some tunes or not. Then I added, "I . . . have some originals I'd like you to hear."

Julian nodded his head slowly in surprise when he heard that. "Really? You want to play me some of your own tunes?"

I nodded my head slowly in return.

"That's big."

I raised my eyebrows—in an Abernathy kind of way—that said, *Yeah, for me, it is.*

Julian frowned suddenly. "Don't take this the wrong way, Regina. 'Cause I really, really want to hear your songs."

Oh, no. What was Julian going to say? What could be more important? Julian let the moment hang, then said, "It's *so beautiful* outside. Want to take a walk first? Before it all gets spoiled?"

A deep, inner sigh of relief. A huge, outer smile of happiness. What a wonderful idea!

I told Julian I'd love to take a walk in the snow with him, so we put on our jackets and boots and went outside where everything was fresh and beautiful and new and white. It reminded me of that *Calvin and Hobbes* comic where they go outside after a big snowfall.

Hobbes says, "Everything familiar has disappeared! The world looks brand-new!"

Calvin says, "A new year . . . a fresh, clean start!"

Hobbes adds, "It's like having a big white sheet of paper to draw on!"

Calvin exclaims, "A day full of possibilities!" Then he adds, "It's a magical world, Hobbes, ol' buddy . . . let's go exploring!"

And that's exactly what Julian and I did.

Thank you for reading this FEIWEL AND FRIENDS book.
The Friends who made

THE GIRL WHO BECAME
A BEATLE

possible are:

Jean Feiwel
publisher

Liz Szabla
editor-in-chief

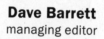

Rich Deas
creative director

Elizabeth Fithian
marketing director

Holly West
assistant to the publisher

Dave Barrett
managing editor

Nicole Liebowitz Moulaison
production manager

Ksenia Winnicki
publishing associate

Anna Roberto
editorial assistant

Find out more about our authors and artists and our
future publishing at www.feiwelandfriends.com.

OUR BOOKS ARE FRIENDS FOR LIFE